UNFAIR WARNING

Clint opened the stall gate and walked through. Still unsure of what to do, the three men backed away.

"Now wait a minute," the first man said. "You can't just mount up and ride out of here."

"Okay." Clint sighed. "Let's get this over with."

"W-whataya mean?" the first man asked.

"You were sent here to do a job," Clint said. "What was it?"

Nobody answered.

"To scare me?"

"To hurt me?"

Blank stares.

"To kill me?"

No answer.

"Why don't we just do this?" Clint said. "If you were sent to scare me, you haven't. If you were sent to hurt me, that's not going to happen. And if you were sent to kill me . . .

"Well, then, have at it . . ."

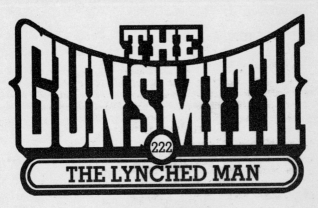

THE GUNSMITH

222

THE LYNCHED MAN

J. R. ROBERTS

JOVE BOOKS, NEW YORK

This is a work of fiction. Names, characters, places, and incidents are either the product of the author's imagination or are used fictitiously, and any resemblance to actual persons, living or dead, business establishments, events, or locales is entirely coincidental.

THE LYNCHED MAN

A Jove Book / published by arrangement with
the author

PRINTING HISTORY
Jove edition / June 2000

The Penguin Putnam Inc. World Wide Web site address is
http://www.penguinputnam.com

ISBN: 0-515-12840-6

A JOVE BOOK®
Jove Books are published by The Berkley Publishing Group,
a division of Penguin Putnam Inc.,
375 Hudson Street, New York, New York 10014.
JOVE and the "J" design
are trademarks belonging to Penguin Putnam Inc.

PRINTED IN THE UNITED STATES OF AMERICA

10 9 8 7 6 5 4 3 2 1

ONE

It took Clint Adams exactly five minutes after he rode into French Creek to find out that there was no creek, and that no one there had ever even seen a live Frenchman.

"Helluva nice name for a town, though, ain't it?" the liveryman asked.

"It sure is," Clint said.

French Creek was in Minnesota. Clint didn't like Minnesota—some bad things had happened to some friends of his named James and Younger, there—but the town was actually *just* in Minnesota by a few miles, right in the Southeasternmost corner so that Iowa and Nebraska were just a quick getaway away.

He was only there to look at a horse. For the past few months, since his beloved black gelding, Duke, had been put out to pasture, he had been searching for a replacement, following up rumors or promises every chance he got. This one was a promise. A friend of his named Artemus Bates promised him that he had just the horse for him.

"Do you know Artemus Bates?" Clint asked the liveryman.

"Who?"

1

Clint repeated the name.

"Sounds familiar," the man said, scratching his bald head, which was covered with brown spots. "What's he do?"

"He's got a place near here, I think," Clint said.

"A ranch?"

"A house, anyway," Clint said. "Don't know if it's a ranch."

"Friend of yours?"

"Yes."

"And you don't know if he's got a ranch?"

"I've never been there," Clint said. "I'm supposed to go there and look at a horse."

"This ain't exactly prime country to raise horses in, ya know," the liveryman said.

"I know," Clint said. "He heard I was looking for a horse, and said he had one for me to look at. I don't know if he actually has a ranch and raises horses."

"Well, if he did, I'd know it," the man said, "so I guess he don't."

"I'll ask somebody else if they know him."

"Might try the sheriff," the man said. "It's his damn job to know everybody, ain't it?"

"That's part of it, I guess."

"What's the matter with this horse?" the man asked, looking at the rangy roan Clint was turning over to him.

"Just won't do it for me in the long run," Clint said. "I had a good horse for a long time, but he's been put out to pasture and I'm looking for a replacement."

"This one looks fine to me," the man said, eyeing the roan critically.

"Well," Clint said, "if my friend does have a horse for me, maybe I'll sell you this one."

"You let me know, then," the man said.

Clint collected his rifle and saddlebags before the man

walked the horse into the livery and got directions to the nearest decent hotel.

"They got a dining room," the man said, "and the other one don't."

"Two hotels in town?"

"That's all," the liveryman said, "and a couple of rooming houses, but you're better off at the one I give ya, the Frenchman's House."

"But no Frenchman, huh?"

"Not as long as I been livin' here."

"And how long's that?"

"Too damn long," the man said, and walked the roan inside the stable.

Clint turned and started back toward the center of town where the Frenchman's House apparently was.

The hotel was pretty easy to spot. It had two floors, easily the biggest building on that part of the street. Farther down and across the street there was a similar building with a sign that read Frenchman's Saloon.

He entered the hotel and welcomed the warmth in the lobby. It wasn't winter anymore, but this was still Minnesota. The cold was another reason he didn't like it here much.

"Help ya?" the clerk asked.

"I'd like a room."

"For how long?"

"A couple of days ought to do it."

"Sign in, then," the man said. He was tall and gangly, long-necked with thick lips and small eyes.

"Why's this place called Frenchman House?" Clint asked, signing the register.

"Ain't my place to name it or question it," the man said. "You got room six, top of the stairs and make a right. You be wantin' a bath?"

"As a matter of fact, yes."

"Hot or cold?"

"Hot."

"When?"

"Ten minutes?"

"Come down here and go down that hall," the man said, pointing. "Door at the end is where you'll find the tub. Hot water'll be there in ten minutes. After that it starts gettin' cold fast."

"I can believe it," Clint said. "I'll be down in time."

"Don't matter to me if you are or ain't," the man said. "Bath'll be ready."

"Much obliged," Clint said, picking up his rifle and saddlebags.

"Part of the service of Frenchman's House," the man said.

"When's the dining room open?"

"Open now," the man said. "Be open until ten. You got plenty of time to take a bath first."

"Thanks again," Clint said.

He went to the stairs, passing the entrance to the dining room as he did. There was no one eating in there at the moment. He hoped it was that empty when he was ready to eat.

TWO

Clint was on time, and as promised the bath water was hot. He languished in the bath for a while before getting out, drying himself and dressing in fresh, clean clothes. Right from there he went to the dining room and, as he had hoped, it was empty. Clint liked eating in empty rooms. He knew no one was going to recognize him. When they did they either stared at him or took a shot at him, and he didn't like either one. He preferred to be able to eat in peace.

He went into the room and a waiter approached him.

"Sir?"

"I'd like a table."

"As you can see," the waiter said, "you can take your pick."

"That one in the back, against the wall."

"This way."

Even in an empty room, though, he preferred to sit with his back to the wall, at a table from which he could see everything. Just because the room was empty didn't mean he had to get careless.

Once he was seated he ordered a pot of coffee and a steak.

"Anything else?" the waiter asked.

"Anything that comes with the steak," Clint said. He would have been happy just with the coffee and steak, but he'd gladly take any extras.

"Coming up."

The waiter was younger than the liveryman and the desk clerk, the youngest man he'd seen in town, so far. In fact, as he'd ridden down the main street he hadn't seen many people at all, and those he did see he didn't get a good look at.

The waiter returned with his coffee and Clint took a good look at his face. He appeared to be in his twenties, while the desk clerk had looked forty and the liveryman sixty.

"What kind of town would you say this is?" Clint asked him.

"The kind I want to get out of," the young man said.

"It's got a pretty name."

"It's a stupid name," the waiter said. "There ain't no creek and ain't nobody French in town."

"Why are the hotel and the saloon called the French-man?"

"Gotta ask the owner that."

"And who's the owner?"

"My boss," the waiter said, eyes darting about to see who was watching or listening, "which means I can't talk about him."

"The same fella owns both?"

"Yes, sir," the waiter said. "I got to get your food."

The boy suddenly looked like he thought he had said too much.

"Hey," Clint said, "relax. I'm not going to tell anybody what you said."

"I got to get your food," he said again, and hurried off.

Clint wondered if the young man was simply nervous talking about his boss, or if he was afraid of the man. As curious as he was he decided not to ask the waiter any more questions. At least, not until he had all his food.

The steak was prepared just the way he liked it, and the coffee was hot, but not as strong as he would have liked. The cook had thrown some vegetables on the plate with the meat, and the last thing the waiter brought was a basket of rolls. All in all, it was a decent meal.

"Tell your cook he did a good job," Clint said to the waiter while paying his bill.

"I'll tell 'im."

"Listen," Clint said, "I wasn't trying to get you into trouble, or anything before. I just got to town and I was just curious."

"The bartender over at the saloon loves to talk," the waiter said. "He'll tell ya anythin' you wanna know."

Clint thought that was true of most bartenders, but he said, "Okay. Thanks for the tip."

He left the dining room and walked through the lobby, not attracting the clerk's attention at all, which suited him fine. If he attracted no attention during his whole stay he'd be very happy.

He had a choice when he left the hotel: he could go to the saloon or to the sheriff's office. He decided on the saloon. If he found out what he needed to know from the bartender maybe he could just head to Artemus Bates's place and not have to deal with the local law.

He entered the saloon and although it was about half full no one really looked up at him. The whole town seemed to have the same odd lack of curiosity. As he approached the bar the bartender came over to see what he wanted.

"Help ya?"

"Yeah," Clint said, "I'd like a beer and some information."

"Beer I got," the bartender said.

"And information?"

"Guess that depends on what you want to know," the man replied. "I'll get the beer."

Clint waited until the man returned with a mug of beer, and leaned on the bar with his elbows.

"Now," he said, "about that information?"

"I'm looking for a friend of mine," Clint said, "supposed to have a place somewhere near here."

"What's his name?"

"Bates, Artemus Bates."

"Bates," the barkeep said, rubbing his full beard with a thick-fingered hand. He was not a big man, but he seemed to be thick all over—although the belly might have simply been a result of middle age.

"Artemus," Clint said, again.

"Don't know 'um."

"That's odd," Clint said.

"Oh? Why's that?"

"Because if he lives near here I'm sure he'd be in the saloon almost half the time," Clint said. "He likes saloons."

"Well," the bartender said, "there is another saloon in town, a couple of streets away from here."

"Which way?"

"Out the door, make a right."

"That place wouldn't happen to be owned by the same person as this one and the hotel, would it?"

The man frowned and said, "No, it wouldn't."

"I was told over at the hotel you might answer a question for me."

"More information?"

"Just idle curiosity."

"Okay."

"Why do the hotel and the saloon have the word French-man in the name?" Clint asked.

"Damned if I know," the bartender said, standing up. "You'd have to ask the owner."

He walked away before Clint could ask who the owner was.

THREE

Clint wasn't used to going to a saloon in a strange town and getting only a drink and no information. So far the liveryman and the bartender had never heard of Artemus Bates. Clint tried to remember when he first heard that Bates was living up here. His telegram from the man, which he received while in Labyrinth, Texas, read only: HEARD YOU NEED A HORSE. GOT ONE FOR YOU. COME AND GET HIM. It was signed: "Artemus Bates."

"One of your many friends all over the country?" Rick Hartman had asked.

The telegram had been delivered to Clint while he was in Hartman's saloon, Rick's Place.

"I met Bates about five or six years ago, helped him out of a tight spot," Clint said.

"So he figures he owe you?"

"I guess so."

Hartman laughed.

"How many friends like that do you have across this great land?"

"A few."

"More than a few, I think," Rick said. "How long's he

lived up there, where it's cold?" Rich shivered. He hated the cold, which was why he remained in south Texas.

Clint thought a moment and then said, "I don't know. In fact, I can't even remember where he was living before that."

And he couldn't remember now.

Some friend . . .

This time he decided to go to the law and see what the sheriff knew . . . if anything.

He knocked and entered the sheriff's office. Unlike most of the people he had seen in town and in the saloon, when he entered the sheriff's office the man looked up from his desk.

"Can I help you?" he asked.

Clint couldn't see the man's chest from where he was so he didn't know if this was the sheriff, or a deputy.

"Are you the sheriff?"

"That's me," the man said. "The name's Sheriff Robbins, Jake Robbins. Just get into town?"

"A little while ago," Clint said. "I got myself a room, a bath and a meal—oh, and a drink—and then decided to come over here and introduce myself."

"Why?"

"My name's Clint Adams."

"Oh," the sheriff said, warily, "that's why." He sat back and eyed Clint suspiciously. "What brings you to French Creek, Mr. Adams?"

"I'm looking for someone."

"To kill?"

"What?"

"Are you hunting bounty now?"

"No," Clint said, patiently, "it's nothing like that. I'm looking for a friend who's supposed to be living somewhere near here."

"Oh," Robbins said, although he still didn't look very convinced. "What's his name?"

"It's Bates, Artemus Bates. He's supposed to have a house or a ranch up here, someplace."

"Bates," the sheriff repeated. "Can't say I know the name."

"Is there another town near here?"

"There's small town called Benson's Fork about fifty miles north of here. After that you'd have to go to Sioux Falls. That's a lot bigger than Benson's—hell, it's a lot bigger than we are, too."

Clint wondered if there were any Sioux near it, or if there was even a falls in the vicinity.

Clint had sent one telegram back to Bates, and gotten one reply in return. It read: NEAR THE BORDER, CLOSE TO FRENCH CREEK.

"No," Clint said, "he specifically mentioned this town and said he didn't live far from the border."

"Well, we're the first town you come to in Minnesota," Robbins said, "but I sure don't know the name. When did he move here?"

"I'm not sure," Clint said, then added, "actually, I don't know, Sheriff."

"Well," the lawman said, "must have been real recent. Did you check with the bartender at the saloon?"

"I talked to the one at the Frenchman," Clint said. "I guess I better go and talk to the other one."

"Bartenders usually know more than anybody," the sheriff said, "even local lawmen."

"That's what I thought, too," Clint said. "Well, thanks anyway."

"Wish I coulda helped. How long you figure on bein' in town—not that I'm rushin' you, or anything."

"Well, originally I figured a couple of days might do it," Clint said. "Now I don't know. Before I can look at the horse he said he had for me, I've got to find him, don't I?"

"Guess ya do," the sheriff said. "Good luck."

Clint left the sheriff's office thoroughly puzzled. Had he read the telegrams wrong? No, the key operator distinctly told him that the telegrams came from Minnesota. Wait . . . did French Creek even have a telegraph office? He couldn't remember seeing the wires when he rode in, but then he wasn't looking. If French Creek did have a key, then somebody in town must know Bates. If it didn't have a key, then he had to have gone somewhere else to send it. Sioux Falls certainly sounded like a big enough town to have a telegraph key. If he sent it from there, though, that really didn't help. He would have ridden there, sent it, waited for a reply, sent his own reply and then headed back home.

He had to live somewhere between French Creek and Sioux Falls—and that's where Benson's Fork was.

He wondered if there was a fork near the town, or if there was even someone living there named Benson?

FOUR

Clint checked in with the bartender at the other saloon, which had a more traditional name to it: the Lady Gay Saloon. It was smaller than the Frenchman, and only about a quarter full at a time of day when a saloon should be packed.

"Artemus Gates, you say?" the man asked.

"Bates," Clint said, "the last name is Bates."

"Well," the bartender said, sticking the tip of the small finger of his left hand in his ear and wriggling it around, "Gates or Bates, I can't say I remember anyone by either name."

"Maybe somebody else would remember him?"

The bartender, a burly man in his fifties, shrugged and said, "Ask around, if you want. Did you check at the Frenchman? Bigger place than us, you'll find more people there."

"I was in there earlier," Clint said, "but I'll go back when I'm done here."

"Sure," the man said, "you'll find a lot of people there now, maybe somebody remembers your friend."

"I hope so . . ."

15

• • •

But nobody did. No one at the Lady Gay did, and when he went back to the Frenchman to ask around there he came up empty again. The Lady Gay had no saloon girls, but the Frenchman did, and he checked with them, because Bates liked women a lot—especially saloon girls.

Of the three girls who worked in the Frenchman none of them remembered Bates, but all three invited Clint to go upstairs with them. He declined and they all told him to let them know if he changed his mind.

They were all attractive, and under other circumstances he might have made arrangements for later, if there was no money involved, but he was still determined to find somebody who knew Artemus Bates.

He walked around town, but it was late and many of the businesses had closed. He was passing the sheriff's office when the door opened and the man stepped out.

"Comin' to see me?" he asked.

"No," Clint said, "just passing by." But he wondered if the sheriff had been looking out the window and deliberately stepped out now to "run in" to him.

"Find anyone who knows your friend?" Sheriff Jake Robbins asked.

"Nope," Clint said, "no one."

"What do you plan to do, then?"

"I'll take a ride tomorrow, see if I can find his place," Clint said. "After that I guess I'll have to find wherever he sent me the telegrams from."

"That'd be Sioux City," Robbins said. "Closest place to us that has a telegraph key."

"That's what I thought," Clint said. "I also thought I might run into his place between here and there."

"You'll run into Benson's Fork, first," Robbins said. "Maybe somebody there will know him."

"I'll check," Clint said. "I'm just taking a walk around

town now. I'll probably end up in the Frenchman's Saloon later."

"I'll see you there, then," Robbins said. "I stop in there on my rounds."

"I'll buy you a drink, then."

"I'll take you up on that."

Clint stood on the boardwalk in front of the sheriff's office and watched the man walk away. What were the chances, he wondered, that the sheriff was lying to him? What were the chances that the entire town was lying? No, how could that be? For one thing, he'd never known that many people to be able to agree on anything, so how could they agree on a lie? And why would they lie?

He shook his head, turned and walked the other way. One more turn around town and then back to the saloon to find a way to entertain himself until he was ready to turn in. Then up early the next morning to take a ride around the area and see if he could find Bates's place.

He would prefer that to having to ride deeper into Minnesota to Sioux Falls. He had the feeling that the farther into Minnesota he got, the colder it was going to get.

FIVE

Clint woke the next morning with a bare butt pressed up against his hip. He turned his head and looked at the girl lying in bed next to him. It was one of the saloon girls, but which one? There were three, two blondes and one brunette. The blondes were both short and full-bodied, and Clint had suspected they were sisters. They were built the way he liked women to be built—for bed. The brunette was tall and slender, with small, high breasts and long, slim legs. Not the way he usually liked his bedmates to be built, but as he looked over at her now he saw her dark hair fanned out over the pillow. She was lying with her back to him, and her neat little bottom was warm against his hip and thigh—and he remembered.

When he returned to the Frenchman's Saloon he ordered a beer and leaned on the bar. He looked around the place, didn't see any poker games going on, so he figured he'd nurse a beer, finish it, and then return to his hotel room. That's when the brunette came up next to him, and that's when he took his first real good look at her face.

She was very beautiful, had eyes a color he had never

seen before. Not blue, really, not green . . . he couldn't describe them but combined with a wide mouth and high cheekbones it was an exotically beautiful face that was hard to take your eyes off of.

"Hi," she said.

"Hi."

"We met earlier," she said. "You were asking me and the other two girls about your friend?"

"I remember," he said. "Are they sisters?"

"Tracy and Reggie?"

"Reggie?"

"Regina," she said. "No, they're not sisters, but they do look alike, don't they?"

"Very much."

"Anyway, my name is Lily."

"Clint."

"Hi, Clint," she said. "I still don't know who your friend is, but I'm so bored with the men in this town . . ."

"Meaning?"

"Meaning that, if you don't mind, I'd like to stand by you until closing time so that they'll all stay away from me."

"Isn't it your job to mingle with them?"

"I'm tired of mingling with them," she said. "I'm tired of doing everything and anything with them, if you get my meaning."

"I think I do."

"If you'll buy me a drink I'll nurse it the way you're nursing yours," she said. "I promise you won't have to buy me another."

"That wouldn't be a problem."

"I just don't want you to think I'm just trying to get you to spend money on me," she said.

"Okay," he said. "What happens after we finish our drinks?"

"What were you going to do after you finished yours?"

"Go to my hotel room and get some sleep."

"Fine," she said, "I'll go with you."

"But, I wouldn't want to pay—"

"You wouldn't have to pay me for anything," she said. "I got that message before, you know, that you don't like to pay."

"Oh."

"No," she said, "I'll just go to your room with you and spend the night."

"The night?"

"Yeah," she said. "You know . . . sleep?"

"Oh," he said, "sleep."

"That is, if you don't mind me sleeping in the same bed with you?" she asked.

"Well, no," he said, "that wouldn't be a problem, but . . ."

"But what?"

"I, uh, what if . . . you know, after we got into bed . . . to go to sleep . . . what if, uh . . ."

"What if you decided you wanted me?"

"Well . . . yeah, that's one way to put it."

"Why?" she asked, stepping back one step. "Do I appeal to you?"

"Of course you do."

"Why?"

"You're very beautiful."

"But not your type."

"Lily," he said, "you're any man's type, and you know it."

"Maybe I just wanted to hear you say it."

"Well, you are."

"Will you buy me that drink?" she asked. "I mean, to start with?"

"Sure."

He called the bartender over and she said, "Beer."

When she had it she took a little sip and licked the suds off her upper lip, which Clint found very arousing.

"Uh-oh," she said.

"What?"

"You want me already," she said. "I can see it in your eyes."

"Uh, well . . ."

"Look" she said, "you're doing me a favor by sort of helping me take a night off from all . . . this . . ." she said, waving her arm. "So, the least I could do—if you let me come back to your room—is let you have me."

"Let me have you?"

"I mean, if you wanted to, uh, have me."

"Well, I . . ."

"I mean, I wouldn't mind . . ."

They stared at each other for a few moments, and then he said, "Why don't we just see what happens when we get to my room?"

"Okay," she said. "It's a deal."

And this was what had happened, he thought, looking down at her.

SIX

Clint pulled the bedclothes down so he could see her back, and her butt. She was thin, but she had a nice bottom, shaped sort of like a peach. She smelled good, tasted good—everywhere!—and was very eager in bed. And he still couldn't quite get the color of her eyes.

He ran his hand down her thin back until he could stroke the cleft between her cheeks with his finger. She moaned and moved her bottom back against his hand. He stroked each cheek, squeezing it, then slid his hand around in front of her, over her flat belly and then down into the dense forest of her pubic hair. He stroked her there until she was wet, then slid a finger into her. She moaned and wriggled and finally turned onto her back.

Her breasts were so small they almost disappeared when she was on her back, but she had the prettiest nipples. She smiled at him and he leaned over to kiss her, his hand still touching her. He moved his lips over her neck, then down to her breasts so he could kiss each nipple. Then he moved up and kissed her pretty mouth, again, and then again.

She licked his lips, bit the bottom one, sucked it into her mouth and then slid her hand between his legs to stroke him while he continued to stroke her.

"Good morning," she said.

"Good morning."

"So I guess we've established that you did want me last night."

"Yes, we did."

"Good."

She rolled over so that her thighs closed over his busy hand. At the same time she ran her hand up and down his erect penis, pausing every so often to rub the ball of her thumb on the spot just beneath the head, on the underside, where she knew it was very sensitive. She had investigated the spot very thoroughly during the night with her tongue; that was how she knew he was *very* sensitive there.

She rolled over again, moving atop him, forcing him to remove his hand. She slithered down between his legs and started using her mouth on him again. She was extremely good at this and he just laid back and gave himself up to the sensations of her mouth and tongue on him.

She sucked him into her mouth and began to wet him thoroughly. When she was satisfied with how wet he was she released him, squatted over him and took him inside of her. She remained in a squat, with all her weight on her legs, and began to ride him up and down that way. He marvelled at how much strength she seemed to have in those slender legs.

She rode him like that until she literally sucked his seed from him. He groaned and then yelled as he finished erupting inside of her and then she released him and collapsed on her back next to him.

"That's a good way to wake up," she said.

"I don't think you're quite awake enough, yet."

"Wha—"

He got down between her legs and started to return the favor. She had a lot of hair there, which he didn't mind at all. He liked the way it felt on his palm as he rubbed his hand over her, then he probed through the hair with his tongue until he touched her wetness, making her jump and moan. He began to work on her in earnest, then using his lips and tongue on her. She reached down and put both hands on his head to hold him there and then lifted her butt and started grinding herself against his face. As he brought her closer and closer to completion she began to moan, and then almost growl at him. He felt her belly begin to tremble, and then her thighs closed on him as she was overtaken by waves of pleasure, crying out loud enough for the whole hotel—hell, the entire town—to hear her . . .

"Now you're awake," he said, moments later.

"Oh, yessss . . ." she said, stretching her body so taut that she seemed to have no breasts at all, just those big, sexy nipples.

"And hungry?"

"Mmmm?"

"I asked if you were hungry?"

"I don't know," she said. "I can't tell. I'm still numb. How did you get so damned good at that?"

"Practice," he said.

She laughed and said, "And a lot of happy women, I bet."

"Are you sure you're not hungry?"

"No," she said, shaking her head, "not hungry."

Her eyes were closed.

"Well, I'm hungry," he said, swinging his feet to the floor. "I'm going downstairs for breakfast."

"You're amazing," she said. "After what we did most men would be fast asleep again."

"I guess it doesn't make them hungry."

"I can't eat, yet," she said, and turned over on her side, presenting him with her firm little butt, again.

He ran his hand over it, then slapped her left cheek hard enough to make her yelp.

"Still not hungry!" she cried out.

"Okay, then," he said, standing up. "You stay here and I'll go downstairs and get something to eat."

"That sounds like a deal."

By the time he finished dressing he could tell by her breathing that she was asleep again. He covered her gently with the sheet, so as not to wake her up, and then slipped out the door.

SEVEN

When he got down to the dining room there were a few people there eating. At one table was a man eating alone, and at another a middle-aged couple. The young waiter recognized him as he sat at the same table as the day before.

"Relax," Clint said, "I'm not going to ask you any questions this time. Just bring me some steak and eggs and we'll be done."

"Yes, sir."

The waiter seemed very relieved that Clint wasn't going to ask him any more questions. Clint still hadn't found out the name of the person who owned the Frenchman's House and the Frenchman's Saloon. His curiosity would have to go unsatisfied for a while longer, though. Right after breakfast he was going to take the roan out and see if he could find Artemus Bates's place. If he didn't, then he was going to have to leave the next day and head for Sioux City. That annoyed him because he could have used a couple of days of getting even better acquainted with Lily.

Still, he could always stop into French Creek again on his way back. The warmest place he'd ever been in Minnesota was that hotel bed with Lily.

27

The waiter brought his breakfast and hurried off as if afraid Clint would break his word about asking more questions. This fueled his curiosity again about who owned the hotel and saloon and he decided he would ask Lily when he saw her again later in the day.

He reclaimed the roan from the livery and headed out. He did not ride north, for he would be doing that if and when he had to go to Sioux City. Neither did he ride south, because he had come from that direction. So he started with east, figuring to spend the morning checking that, and the afternoon checking west. He even brought some beef jerky with him for when he got hungry.

He came to several homesteads east of town but when he stopped to inquire none of them were owned by Artemus Bates. Likewise, none of the people had ever heard of Bates. He did not find anything that remotely resembled a ranch.

Later in the afternoon he also found several homes west of town, but again none of them were owned by, or even knew of, Artemus Bates.

It was getting more and more curious.

He stayed out until late afternoon, and by this time his beef jerky was gone, as was almost all his water. Hunger drove him to head back to town and admit that a trip to Sioux City was going to be necessary.

He was a few miles out of town when he heard the shot. He threw himself from the saddle a split second before the bullet would have struck him in the back. It was only his keenly developed sense of self-preservation that allowed him to act during that millisecond between the sound of the rifle being fired and the arrival of the bullet. It missed him, but it didn't miss the horse. The bullet struck the animal in the back of the head, killing it instantly. The animal fell and Clint had to scramble again to keep from being crushed by the thousand-pound animal. At the same time he drew his gun and looked around for the shooter, hoping to locate him before he made the necessary adjustment and fired again.

But there was no adjustment, and no second shot, which led Clint to the immediate conclusion that he was not dealing with a professional.

He waited several more seconds before moving again. He stood and walked warily over to where the horse was lying. It took him only a moment to ascertain that the animal was dead. He also determined that for the bullet to have missed him and struck the horse the way it did it had to have been fired from above. Since there were no hills, rises or mountains nearby that meant that somebody was up in a tree. That also meant they had to get back down again after missing, and quickly. If he still had the use of his horse he might have been able to move fast enough to catch them. As it was now he simply stood in place and looked around, hoping to see something useful—like somebody shimmying down a tree with a rifle. Unfortunately, he didn't see anyone, or anything.

He holstered his gun and tried to remove his saddlebags, but the horse was lying on one. He was going to need help to get it, and the saddle, off the horse. Luckily, he was only a few miles from French Creek, and he started walking, hoping to make it before nightfall, and before someone else—or the same person—took another shot at him.

During his walk to town he came to two possible conclusions. One was the usual one, that someone had recognized him and tried to make a reputation for themselves, even by shooting him in the back.

The second was that someone didn't want him to find

Artemus Bates, or find out what had happened to Artemus Bates.

He decided that when he got back to town he wouldn't tell anyone about this attempt on his life, not even the sheriff. After all, there was no telling who was behind it. In the morning he would head to Sioux City as planned. It was still important to find out if that was where Bates had sent the telegram from, and if his place was between French Creek and Sioux Falls. He also had to check Benson's Fork. However, from now on he was going to act on the premise that someone did not want him to find Bates, and *that* someone would apparently go to any lengths to accomplish their goal.

EIGHT

He reached town just at nightfall and went directly to the sheriff's office. He'd realized that he'd have to report the incident to the sheriff in order to get help retrieving his saddle and saddlebags from the dead horse. As he entered the office, though, he saw that the man was not there. He decided to go to his hotel to clean up before looking for him further.

"What do you mean you missed?"

Kyle Morgan looked down and said, "I don't know how he did it, but as I fired he jumped from his horse. My bullet killed the horse, but he got away."

"Did you fire a second time?" Morgan's employer asked.

"Well . . ."

"You didn't, did you?" the employer asked. "He was on the ground, wasn't he? You could have fired again."

"He came up with his gun out," Morgan said. "I had to get out of there."

"You fired once, missed, and panicked."

Morgan didn't answer.

"That's what I get for sending an idiot to do a man's job."

"But I—"

"Get out."

Morgan hesitated only a moment, then turned and fled from the room.

This time, his employer thought, I need to find a man who won't panic because his intended target was the Gunsmith. That kind of man could not be found in a town the size of French Creek.

Clint was able to clean up because his fresh shirt was in his room, and not in the saddlebag underneath the dead roan. He knew that if he had been riding Duke somehow the big black gelding would also have come out of the incident alive. The roan did not have Duke's instincts, and suffered because of it.

Now he had the added problem of finding a horse that could take him to Sioux City. It was back to the livery, then, to see if they had one available, even for rent.

But first he had to find the sheriff.

It was more than likely the sheriff was out making his rounds. The man had told him that the saloon was included, and he had even offered to buy him a drink, but the lawman had never showed up the night before. He decided to be there tonight and see if he showed up this time.

When he got to the saloon it was busy. The three girls were working the floor but Lily took a moment to wave at him from across the room. Now that he'd slept with her she looked even more beautiful and he waved back, feeling as if he could still smell her and taste her.

He went to the bar and ordered a beer.

"Has the sheriff been in?" he asked.

"Not yet."

"Does he usually come in here?"

The man nodded and said, "On his rounds."

"I didn't see him last night."

The man shrugged. "Sometimes he misses."

The bartender went away and he turned, beer in hand, to survey the room. No one was looking at him. He wondered if the man who had taken the shot at him was somewhere in that room. If he was, he was doing a really good job of ignoring his intended target. Maybe he was a pro, after all. No, a pro would have taken at least one more shot, not panicked and ran.

He was halfway through his beer when the sheriff entered and walked up to him.

"You ain't been waitin' for me since last night, I hope," the man said, with a smile.

"Just got here a while, myself."

"That offer of a drink still hold?"

"Sure."

The sheriff called the bartender over and ordered a beer. When he had it he turned to face Clint.

"Find anything out today?"

"Yeah, I did."

"What's that?"

"Somebody doesn't want me to find Artemus Bates."

"What makes you say that?"

"Somebody took a shot at me while I was heading back to town," he said. "Shot my horse out from under me. I had to walk back to town."

The sheriff stopped with his beer halfway to his mouth and lowered it.

"When was this?"

"A little while ago," he said. "I just got back around nightfall."

"Did you see who it was?"

"No," Clint said. "They took one shot, missed, and ran."

"Not a professional, then."

"No."

"What makes you think this has anything to do with your friend?" the sheriff asked. "No offense, but I bet you get shot at all the time."

"No offense taken," Clint said, "and you're right, I do, but this just doesn't feel like one of those times. Too much coincidence. No, I think something's going on and my friend has gotten himself right in the middle of it."

"So what are you going to do?"

"Well, first I'll need some help getting my gear off the dead horse and back to town."

"That's no problem," Robbins said. "I'll get somebody and we'll go out there with you tomorrow."

"Next, I've got to find another horse."

"Hmm, I don't know if anyone in French Creek has a horse to sell."

"I'd rent one," Clint said. "I just want to go to Sioux City. I'm sure I could buy one there, and then bring the rented one back."

"I suppose that could be arranged. Still going to Sioux City to check the telegraph office?"

"That's right," Clint said, "and to check and see if his place is somewhere between there and here."

"There's a Marshal in Sioux City," Sheriff Robbins said. "You might want to check in with him, also."

"Thanks, I'll do that."

"When do you want to leave?"

"As soon as I collect my gear from the dead horse and rent another one."

"After breakfast okay?"

"That's fine."

The sheriff put his half-finished beer down on the bar.

"I'll see you in the morning, then."

"Okay," Clint said. "I'll be appreciative of your help."

"Don't mention it."

As the sheriff started to leave Clint said, "By the way."

"Yeah?"

"What happened to you last night?" Clint asked. "I *was* going to buy you a drink then."

The sheriff hesitated a moment, then said, "Somethin' came up."

"Oh, well, I guess that happens in your business."

"More than you think," the sheriff said, and left the saloon.

NINE

Once again Clint awoke the next morning with Lily's neat little bottom pressed against him. He snuggled up against her, slid his hand around and began to play with her marvelous nipples. In moments he was on his back with her astride him, the length of him buried inside the steamy depth of her. Sitting on him like this her breasts dangled just a bit, like small pieces of fruit, and he nibbled at them, bringing the nipples fully to life. She rode him hard until they were both wet with perspiration, and then continued to ride him until she had enough . . .

"I hope you don't mind," she said, gasping for air moments later, "but that was for me."

"I didn't mind," he assured her.

"I'll need something to remember you by."

"I told you I'll be back this way," he said. "I'll need to bring back the rented horse."

"Well," she said, "just in case . . ."

"Nothing's going to happen to me, Lily."

"I don't know how you can say that," she argued. "Somebody tried to kill you yesterday, didn't they?"

"Tried," he said, "and failed."

"So they'll probably try again."

"I don't think so," he said. "They took one shot and then ran, and they're probably still running."

"Well then," she said, "consider this added incentive to come back this way."

He smiled, kissed her and said, "That I can do."

He met the sheriff down in the lobby and bought him breakfast.

"Anymore thoughts on what happened last night?" Robbins asked.

"Like what?"

"Maybe you remembered something?"

"Nope," Clint said. "Nothing to remember. The shooter fired once and was gone. He probably hasn't stopped running yet."

"I hope you're right."

"I do have a question for you, though."

"What's that?"

"Who owns this hotel and the saloon across the street?"

Robbins frowned.

"What's that got to do with your friend, and somebody takin' a shot at you?" he asked.

"Nothing," Clint said. "I'm just curious."

"The owner's name is C. K. Healy. Very reclusive."

"Does he live in town?"

"Above the saloon," Robbins said, "but never comes down."

"That's odd."

"Very."

"So why the word Frenchman in the names?"

"That I don't know," Robbins said. "You'll have to ask the owner."

"How do I get to see the owner?"

"I think," the sheriff said, "you need a much better reason than curiosity to do that."

After breakfast they met another man who was going to help them with the horse. The sheriff introduced him as Bill Marks. Marks had the sheriff's horse and a buckboard. Clint climbed on the buckboard and they rode out to where the dead horse was.

Along the way Marks said, "Sheriff says you need to rent a horse."

"That's right."

"I got one you can rent."

"Thanks," Clint said. "When can I see it?"

"When we get back."

"What kind is it?"

"Five-year-old gray mare," Marks said. "You don't mind ridin' a mare, do ya?"

"As long as she gets me to Sioux City and back it's fine with me," Clint answered.

"She'll do that."

"Then unless she's a nag we just have to work out the price."

"She ain't a nag," Marks said, and they discussed price.

When they reached the dead horse all three men slid the saddle from its back and tossed it onto the buckboard. The sheriff took a few moments to look around the area before they started back.

"Was you attached to him?" Marks asked.

"No," Clint said, "I was just riding him until I could find something else. That's actually why I came here. A friend of mine said he had a horse for me to look at. Maybe you know him?"

"What's his name?"

"Artemus Bates?"

Marks swallowed and then said slowly, "No, don't know him."

With everyone in French Creek who had told him this, this was the first time he felt like he was actually being lied to.

TEN

When they got back to town Marks took Clint to show him the gray mare. That was when he found out that Marks owned the livery.

"This is Austin," Marks said, introducing the liveryman Clint had talked to when he first arrived in town.

"We met," Clint said.

"The horse is back here," Marks said.

He followed the man to a stall in the back of the livery.

"Take a look at her."

Clint did, and the mare looked solid enough. He had the feeling she was a little older than the man was letting on, but since he was only renting the animal he let that go.

"She looks good."

"The price is okay?" Marks asked.

"It's fine."

Clint took his money out and paid Marks for the use of the horse.

"You might as well throw your saddle on her now," Marks said. "Austin, bring in that saddle from the buckboard outside!"

"Okay."

"When will you be back?" Marks asked, counting the money again.

"Probably day after tomorrow, if I make Sioux City in one day."

"You should," Marks said. "Don't see no reason why not."

"I might run into a reason on the way," Clint said. "Don't be thinking I ran off with you horse, Marks. I'll definitely be back."

Marks looked at Clint, then looked away and said, "I trust ya."

"Well," Clint said, "I appreciate that."

Austin came in with the saddle and dropped it on the ground. It was pretty obvious he didn't like lugging it around.

"Thanks," Clint said, all the same.

"Uh," Austin grunted. To Marks he said, "I'll unhitch the team," and walked away.

"Well," Marks said, "I guess I'll be seeing you in a few days."

He left and Clint saddled the gray mare and walked her outside. Although she was gray her tail and mane were black. She was an odd looking animal, but she seemed strong enough to take him to Sioux City with no problem.

He mounted her and rode her to the hotel, tied her off outside. He went in and told the clerk he'd be away a few days, but he'd be back.

"Want us to hold your room?"

"I don't think so," Clint said.

"We might get busy."

Somehow, Clint doubted that, but he just said, "I'll take my chances."

"Suit yourself."

He went to his room and retrieved whatever gear he'd

left there, then went outside to find the sheriff waiting by the horse.

"Nice looking animal," he said, leaning on the horse.

"She'll do."

Clint made sure the saddle was cinched on tight, then put his saddlebags and bedroll on.

"I hope you find what you're lookin' for between here and Sioux Falls," Robins said.

"So do I," Clint said.

"What if you don't?"

"What?"

Clint stopped and faced the lawman.

"What if you don't find your friend between here and there?" Robbins asked. "What will you do then?"

"Keep looking."

"Stubborn, huh?"

"More loyal than stubborn when it comes to my friends," Clint said. "If I don't find him between here and Sioux Falls I'll just check out Sioux Falls. And if I don't find any sign of him there, I'll just come right back here."

"To do what? Oh, return the horse?"

"And to keep looking," Clint said, "and looking and looking, and I won't stop looking until I find Artemus Bates, Sheriff."

Clint mounted up and looked down at the lawman.

"And you can take that to the bank."

ELEVEN

Clint had ridden about twenty or so miles north, maybe halfway between French Creek and Sioux City, when he came to a small homestead: a house, a corral, no barn but a lean-to in the back. He had seen a road sign earlier that led him to believe he was now about five miles from Benson's Fork.

He reined the gray mare in and tied her to the corral, then turned and walked toward the house. It had obviously been built buy the homesteader himself, not professionally, but competently done, constructed completely of wood. The same hand had probably built the corral.

"Hello, the house!" he shouted. He was pretty sure nobody was there, but he didn't want any surprises. He waited and when there was no answer he moved to the front door and knocked. As he did it swung away, held only by one hinge. One look at the lock told him that the door had been kicked in, and the damage looked recent.

He entered and looked around. The house had been simply furnished, but most of those furnishings were now in pieces. Whoever had forced their way in had done so angrily, judging from the amount of damage that had been done.

There was another room, a bedroom, and that had also been ransacked. If this was Artemus Bates's house he had really gotten somebody angry at him—but angry enough to kill?

From all appearances a woman's touch was missing from the place, and he had not heard that his friend had ever married. Also, there was no telling if the owner of the house was even home when the damage was done. There was no blood to be seen anywhere in the house.

He left the house and walked to the corral. Judging from the horse manure on the ground it had been recently occupied by perhaps six or eight animals. Had whoever wrecked the house also stolen the horses? And was there among them the horse Bates had been holding for him?

The last thing he checked was the lean-to. It, too, showed evidence of recent occupancy by a horse. At least one animal had been kept from the others for some reason.

He walked the ground around the house. From what he could see on the ground there had been four of five horses in front of the house, horses shod and ridden. That meant that the damage had been done by at least that many men. He wondered why such anger had not led to actually burning the house down? Had there been among these men a cool enough head to prevent that?

He was done here. He had gleaned as much as he could from what had been left behind. It was time to move on, but to Benson's Fork or Sioux City? He decided to keep heading for Sioux City, where he could have a conversation with the town marshal. Maybe the man knew something about what had happened here.

Hopefully, someone in Sioux City had heard of Artemus Bates.

When he rode into Sioux City he saw that he was in a major town. There were more than a few hotels, saloons, merchants, and an obvious telegraph line. The livery stable had a huge corral behind it, and it was presently filled with horses. He wondered if any of those horses had come from the corral at the deserted and wrecked homestead?

At any rate, the presence of all those horses at least meant that there'd be one available for him to purchase, but that would come later. First he had to talk with the law.

He left the mare in the hands of the liveryman, obtained directions to the marshal's office, and headed there on foot. He left behind his rifle and saddlebags. His plans for the night were unsure.

There was a plaque outside the marshal's office that read MARSHAL JOHN W. DEAN. He had never heard of the man, but anyone who displayed their name that prominently obviously thought a lot of it.

He knocked and entered the office. There was a large desk with a gray-haired man behind it, wearing a blue shirt and a black leather vest. Hanging on a hook on the wall behind him was a black Stetson. The man was cleanly shaved and freshly clipped, and there was the smell of bay rum in the air. Right off the bat Clint pegged this lawman as more politician than anything else.

"Can I help you?" the man asked.

"You can if you're Marshal Dean."

"I am. And who might you be, sir?" the Marshal asked standing up. He was tall, square-shouldered and narrow-hipped.

"My name is Clint Adams."

"The Gunsmith?" Dean seemed delighted. He stuck his hand out and pumped Clint's hand enthusiastically. "It's a real pleasure, sir, a pleasure."

"Thank you, Marshal."

Reluctantly, the lawman released his hand.

"Please, have a seat and tell me how I can help you."

"Well, Marshal," Clint said, sitting across from the man, "I passed a homestead on the way here that was pretty well torn up. I've been looking for a friend of mine who is supposed to be living up here somewhere, and I'm hoping that wasn't his place I passed."

"Hmm. Tell me exactly where this place is?"

Clint described the location of the homestead in relation to both French Creek and Sioux City.

"I think I know the place you mean," Marshal Dean said, "and if you're friends with the man who lived there I'm afraid you won't find much of a welcome here in Sioux City."

"And why's that?"

"Because he raped and killed a teenage girl."

Clint felt a coldness in the pit of his stomach.

"And what happened to him?"

"Well," Dean said, "I'm afraid he was hung."

TWELVE

"Was his name Artemus Bates?"

"We never identified him by name," the Marshal said.

"How could that be? You hung him!"

The Marshal had the good grace to look embarrassed.

"Look, I wasn't there. A bunch of men rode out to his place, ransacked it, and strung him up from a nearby tree. By the time I got there it was all over."

"And what about the men who did it?"

"Never identified them, either," Dean said. He spread his hands in a gesture of helplessness. "Naturally, no one has come forward to claim responsibility."

"No one saw them?" Clint demanded.

"There were those who saw a group of men. None were close enough to identify them. They either can't, or they won't. One man did see them, but he said they had their faces covered."

"Like cowards."

"Like concerned citizen who have children of their own."

"A lynch mob!"

"Yes," Dean said, "and if I could identify them I would arrest them—even though I sympathize with them. The

49

rape and murder was a brutal one, and the girl was only fourteen."

"But how do you know for sure this man did it?"

"He was identified as having been seen talking to the girl."

"That's it?"

Again, Dean spread his hands.

"I'm sorry, Mr. Adams, but I did all I could do."

"Did you talk to the accused man?"

"I did."

"And you didn't ask his name?"

"He wouldn't tell me," Dean said. "He made some rude remarks and refused to answer my question."

"And that made him guilty?"

"It made him *seem* suspicious."

"And that was enough to hang him on?"

"He wasn't from around here," the Marshal said. "He had moved here only about six or eight months before this all happened."

"And when *did* this happen?"

"About two weeks ago."

It had easily taken two weeks from the time Clint got the first telegram until he was able to get a horse and get to Minnesota. The time frame fit, but he still didn't know if the hanged man had been Artemus Bates.

"I'm sorry if it was your friend," Dean said.

"I don't know if it was my friend, Marshal," Clint said. "Can you describe the man to me?"

"Mid-forties, I think, not very tall . . . sort of average, I'm afraid."

"That description could fit anyone."

"Does it fit your friend?"

"Yes."

"Perhaps you should talk to the undertaker," the Marshal said. "He could tell you more about the, uh, body."

That wouldn't help Clint. He wasn't close enough friends with Bates to know about any distinguishing marks that might have been on his body.

"I still don't understand this, Marshal," he said. "You're the law in this town and yet you accuse a man of a rape/murder without being able to identify him, and before you can even gather evidence against him he's dragged out and hung because he was seen with the girl."

"Unfortunately," the Marshal said, "that's pretty much the way it happened, Mr. Adams."

"Did people in Benson's Fork and French Creek know about this?" Clint asked.

"I'm sure the news must have spread to there."

Did the people in French Creek know about it? Was that why everyone denied knowing Bates? But then the "killer" hadn't been identified. That meant they wouldn't have recognized the name "Artemus Bates."

Or would they?

Clint shook his head. There was too much information coming in and he needed time to deal with it. It was beginning to look like a stay in Sioux City was in order.

"I think I'll get a room at one of the hotels, Marshal," he said, standing up, "and think about this, for a while."

"I'm sorry I can't be more helpful, Mr. Adams," the Marshal said. "It must be hard not knowing for sure if it's really your friend we're talking about."

"I assume the incident was carried in your newspaper?"

"Oh, yes," Dean said. "The original incident—the, ah, murder—and then the, uh, hanging."

Lynching, Clint thought. The man didn't seem to want to use that specific word, but that's what it was. What Clint would like to have known was if the Marshal had really been unable—or unavailable—to stop it, or if he'd simply looked the other way. To interfere might have been stepping on the toes of too many potential future voters, and what was the life of one stranger, more or less, when measured against the future political career?

"Thanks for your help, Marshal." Clint shook Marshal John W. Dean's hand when what he really wanted to do was take a poke at the man. Landing himself in jail, though, wouldn't do anybody any good.

"Stop in and see me again while you're in town," Dean said, "just in case I can help."

"I will," Clint said. "If I find out anything, and I need any help, you'll be the first to know."

THIRTEEN

When Clint left the marshal's office it was to go to a hotel and get a room, but he found himself in need of a drink. He went to the nearest saloon—the Black Oak Saloon—went to the bar and ordered a whiskey. He downed it, then ordered a beer. He lingered over that in the half-filled saloon, thinking about what he'd found out. Someone had been lynched, supposedly for raping and killing a teenage girl. Whether or not it was Artemus Bates was something he was going to have to find out.

He turned with half his beer left in his hand and looked around the room. The ceilings were high, the floors bare wood, but the bar was expensive and the tables were decent. The girls were dressed in decent, low-cut gowns designed to show lots of shoulder and breast and sell drinks, and there were gaming tables around. If he'd been there simply for pleasure this would have been the kind of place he would look for it in. As it was he realized that if he started asking questions about the lynching there were probably six men in that room who would be willing to do the same to him just to shut him up.

Suddenly, the beer tasted flat and he left to get himself a hotel room.

•   •   •

He went to the livery first to make arrangements for the horse to be kept a few days, then grabbed his saddlebags and rifle and started for a hotel. The first one he came to was called the Perry Hotel, and looked as good as any. He went in and got a room without drawing a reaction from the desk clerk as he signed in. That was good. Of course, the marshal knew he was in town, so word could have gotten around that way. He'd find out in a matter of hours, if and when people started looking at him funny as he walked the streets or entered a saloon or café.

He stopped in his room only long enough to drop off his belongings and then left to find the undertaker and the newspaper office, not necessarily in that order. He'd stop into the first one he came to.

It was the newspaper.

On the window was stencilled THE SIOUX CITY GAZETTE, and underneath that it read PUBLISHED DAILY.

He went inside and waited for the noise of the press to die down and for someone to notice him. Finally it happened. The press quieted and the man running it turned to him and asked, "Can I help you?"

He was in his thirties, with black hair, intelligent eyes, and a big ink smudge on the tip of his nose.

"I'd like to see some back issues of the paper, if I could?" Clint asked.

"Well, sure," the man said. "How far back do you want to go?"

"Just a couple of weeks."

The man grabbed a rag and started wiping his hands, stepped away from the printing press.

"You just ride in?"

"A little while ago."

"Heard about it already, huh?"

"About what?"

"The murder?"

"Yeah, I heard."

"And you want to read about it?"

"That's right."

"How'd you hear about it?"

"From the marshal."

"You a friend of his?"

"No, but I checked in with him when I got to town."

Now the man frowned, sensing something.

"What's your name?"

"Clint Adams."

The man tossed the rag aside and stuck out his hand.

"Henry Clarence," he said, as Clint shook his hand.

"You run the press?"

"The press, the whole paper," Clarence said. "It's mine.
I know who you are, Mr. Adams."

"I thought you might," Clint said, "seeing as how you're
a newspaperman."

"I'd like to do an interview with you while you're in
town."

"I don't think that'll be possible."

"We could do it at your convenience."

"Does my getting a look at back issues depend on it?"

"No," Clarence said. "I'll get those for you. Have a seat
at that table over there. I'll be right back."

Clint went to the table Clarence had indicated and sat
down. In just a matter of moments Clarence appeared with
a stack of papers.

"I made it easy for you and brought you everything on
the incident. Did you hear about the lynching?"

"I did."

"That's in there, too," Clarence said. "Take your time
reading it. I've got to continue to run the press."

"Okay, thanks."

"We can talk about the interview later, huh?"

"Sure," Clint said, "later."

Henry Clarence nodded and went back to his press. Clint spread the papers out, saw that they all covered the incident on the first page, from the actual discovery of the body to the lynching.

He started to read.

FOURTEEN

All he really got from the newspapers was an explanation of who the girl and her parents were and the fact that Henry Clarence, the editor of the *Sioux City Gazette* was up in arms about the lynching after it happened. He had written an editorial about the unidentified man who hadn't been given a chance to defend himself in a court of law. He decried the lynching of the man and called for federal intervention in finding out who the members of the lynch mob were.

"I see you're up to my editorial," Clarence said, coming up on Clint, wiping his hands on a rag again. Clint hadn't even been aware that the press had stopped running.

"Yes," Clint said. "I read it."

"That's when my staff quit and I had to go through three windows in one week," the man explained.

"Vandals?"

"That's what the marshal tried to convince me," Clarence said, "but I know different."

"I see the little girl's parents are prominent in town."

Clarence snorted and said, "Little girl. Everybody in this town acts like Linda Kendall was a virgin or something."

"Wasn't she fourteen?"

"A very mature fourteen," Clarence said. "That girl had a body that most saloon girls would kill for, and she used it."

"She . . . slept around?"

"Up, down, around, anywhere she could. Of course, that doesn't mean that anyone had the right to rape her," Clarence quickly added, "but I don't seriously think anybody ever had to. She'd drop onto her back and spread her legs for anything in pants. The professional girls in town complained that she was giving it away, and taking away their business."

"And her parents knew?"

"How could they not?" he asked. "But did they admit it? No, never. After she was killed she suddenly became this sainted virgin."

Clint started leafing through the newspapers.

"Did you write that?"

"If I did I wouldn't be here now," Clarence admitted. "I'd have been burned out by now. No, I get outraged sometimes, but I never get stupid."

"Can't blame you for that."

"I got a bottle in my office," Clarence said. "Care for a taste?"

"Sure."

"Thought you might, after reading all that," the editor said. "Follow me."

Clint followed the man into a back office that was totally encased in glass so the man could still see his printing press and "staff," when he had one. He opened his bottom desk drawer, took out a bottle of whiskey, found two glasses, filled them and handed Clint one.

"Now suppose you tell me why you're really interested in this story?" Clarence asked.

Clint hesitated.

"No interview," Clarence went on, "and off the record. What are you really doing here, Mr. Adams?"

"I'm looking for a friend of mine," Clint said. "His name is Artemus Bates, and he's supposed to live around here, someplace—actually, closer to French Creek than here."

"And are you thinking he might be the man they lynched?"

"I'm thinking it's possible," Clint said, "and I'm thinking that if he was, they hung an innocent man."

"Don't think there's anybody in town who doesn't know *that's* true," Clarence said.

"You mean . . . everyone knew he was innocent?"

"Sure."

"Then why'd they hang him?"

"To make the whole thing go away," Clarence said. "To keep anyone from finding out what really happened . . . that's my theory, anyway."

"You don't know any of this for sure, then?"

"No," Clarence said, "just theory. You see, I think rich people have more secrets to hide than poor people do."

"I agree."

"And they use their money to hide them."

"Agreed."

"So I think Allan Kendall—Linda's father—spread some of his money around and made the whole situation go away."

"And what about her mother?"

"Jenny Kendall does what her husband tells her to do or she gets knocked around for her trouble."

"Mr. Clarence—"

"Henry, please."

"Henry," Clint said, "are you trying to tell me that you think this Allan Kendall killed his own daughter? *Raped* and killed his own daughter?"

"First of all," Clarence said, "she wasn't his daughter,

she was his stepdaughter. Second, you got to remember that Linda Kendall waved it under the nose of every man she came in contact with—and that included her stepfather."

"Have you told this theory to anyone else?"

Clarence leaned forward and poured some more whiskey into Clint's glass.

"No. No one would listen, and I'd get myself in a lot of trouble."

"Why are you telling me, then?"

"For two reasons," Clarence said. "The obvious one is because of who you are. The second reason is because you're a stranger. Because of both those reasons I don't think you'll be intimidated by Allan Kendall's money."

"You want me to investigate this for you?"

"You're interested in finding your friend, right?"

"Right."

"So you need to know if the man they lynched was him, right?"

"That's right."

"So you're going to poke around anyway, right?"

"Right again."

Clarence spread his hands and said, "I'm just looking to take a peek over your shoulder, that's all. You see any problem with that?"

Clint drained his glass, held it out and said, "No, I don't."

FIFTEEN

After Clint left the newspaper office he walked to the undertaker's, after obtaining directions from Henry Clarence. However, there was very little the undertaker could tell him. All he knew was that he buried a man whose name he didn't know, who had no particularly distinguishing features or marks on his body—which wouldn't have helped Clint, anyway.

The undertaker said the same thing the marshal had said—the man was just average.

Clint found a café and had lunch. He lingered over it, considering what his next step should be. Would it do any good to go out and talk to the parents of the dead girl? If— as the newspaper editor suspected—there was some kind of cover-up going on, what would he get from them but lies? Still, if they knew that someone was looking into the incident further, maybe they'd make a mistake.

It wasn't hard to find someone to give him directions to the Kendall ranch.

The Kendall spread was impressive. The house was two stories high, the barn huge, the corral next to it was in three sections, and there were men working everywhere. They all stopped to look at him as he rode up to the house, and one man in particular broke away to meet him there.

"Can I help you?" he asked.

"I'd like to see Mr. Kendall."

"I'm the foreman," the man said, folding beefy arms over a barrel chest. "Name's Walker."

"Hello, Mr. Walker," Clint said. "I'd like to see Mr. Kendall."

"Not *Mister* Walker," the man said. "Just Walker."

"I'd still like to see Mr. Kendall."

"What's it about?"

"It's personal."

"Look Mister—" Walker started, then stopped and decided to take another tact, "What's your name?"

"Clint Adams."

He could see the flare of recognition in the man's eyes.

"Wait here," the foreman finally said. "I'll check with Mr. Kendall and find out if he'll see you."

"Thanks."

The foreman turned and entered the house without knocking. Clint was still riding the gray mare he'd rented in French Creek. He dismounted and waited, holding the reins loosely. After a few moments the foreman reappeared, and a man came out the door after him. He was tall, rangy, good-looking, and looked more like a foreman than the foreman did. He came down the stairs with Walker, who stepped aside and folded his arms and the other man fronted Clint.

"I'm Kendall," he said. "Allan Kendall."

"Mr. Kendall, I'm Clint Adams."

"That's what my foreman said," Kendall responded. "How do I know you're really the Gunsmith?"

"Why would I say I was if I wasn't?" Clint asked. "That

would be like painting a bull's-eye on my back."

Kendall studied him for a few moments, then seemed to relax.

"You're right about that," he said. "Walker, have someone see to Mr. Adams's horse."

"Yes, sir."

"Come up on the porch, sir," Kendall said. "We can talk there."

Clint handed the reins to Walker and followed Allan Kendall up the steps to the porch.

"I'm surprised to see you riding such an ordinary horse," Kendall said, when they reached the top. "I'd heard a lot about your black gelding."

"This one is rented," Clint said. "I've been in the market for a new animal for some time."

"What happened to the gelding?"

"He wore out before I did."

"Pity," Kendall said. "Good horses are hard to come by."

"Tell me about it."

"Perhaps while you're here I could show you some," Kendall said. "We have some excellent stock."

"Maybe we'd better wait until I tell you why I'm here," Clint said. "After that you may not want to sell me a horse."

"Business is business," the man said, "but as you wish. I assume you're here about what happened to my daughter."

"Why would you assume that?"

"Am I correct?"

"You are," Clint said, "but I still don't see—"

"Are you a believer in coincidence, Mr. Adams?"

"Not at all."

"Neither am I," Kendall said. "The death of my daughter was an unusual incident, as is your visit. Whether it's a leap of logic or not to assume that was why you are here, I am correct."

"Yes."

"Then perhaps you'd better tell me exactly why you're here," Allan Kendall said, "and we can go on from there."

SIXTEEN

"I'm concerned about the man who was lynched for your daughter's murder," Clint said.

"What about him?"

"I'd like to know who he was."

"So would I," Kendall said, "but he's dead, so there's no chance of finding out, is there?"

"Well, more than that I'd like to find out if he's a friend of mine who I've been looking for," Clint said.

"And who is that?"

"A man named Artemus Bates."

"I never heard of him."

"That's what everyone says," Clint said, "but he lived up here for a certain amount of time. I find it odd that no one in French Creek or Sioux City has heard of him."

"French Creek is a hole," Kendall said. Clint waited for more, but the man stopped there.

"I see," Clint said. "Well, I was wondering if you knew Bates."

"I didn't," Kendall said, "and if he's the man who killed my little girl I'd say he's lucky we weren't introduced."

"See, that's what I want to find out," Clint said. "I can't

believe my friend would have done such a thing, and I
don't think I'm going to be able to leave until I find out
for sure."

"Seems to me there's a very simple way to find out."

"Oh? And how's that?"

"Find your friend," Kendall said. "If you find him alive,
then he wasn't the man, was he?"

"I suppose not," Clint said. "That sounds like good ad-
vice, Mr. Kendall."

Kendall regarded Clint for a moment and then said, "I
really wouldn't want you asking a lot of questions about
what happened."

"Why not?"

"We're trying to put it behind us," the man said, "my
wife and I. It's more difficult for her. Linda was my stepdaughter, you see."

"Yes, I heard that."

"If you start asking questions it's just going to dredge it
all up again," the rancher said.

"Well, you would think that people would want to know
for sure whether or not they hung the right man."

"I'm sure the good people of this community would not
have hung a man without being sure."

"How could they be sure without a trial?" Clint asked.
"Seems to me lynch mobs are always convinced they're
doing the right thing—but they never are."

"I beg to differ," Kendall said. "Sometimes it's the only
way to achieve real justice."

"Vigilante justice, maybe," Clint said, "but not real justice."

"Sometimes," Kendall said, "they are one and the same."

"I'm afraid I have to disagree with you on that count,
Mr. Kendall."

"I wouldn't think a man with your reputation would have
such definite opinions on justice."

"But I do," Clint said. "In fact, I'm a real stickler for justice, which is why I am going to have to stay around and ask a few questions."

"That wouldn't be in your best interests, Mr. Adams."

"Really?" Clint asked. "That sounds an awful lot like a threat, Mr. Kendall."

"Call it whatever you like," Kendall said. "I'm just suggesting you reconsider your plans. This matter is closed."

"Does your wife feel that way?"

Kendall took a quick step toward Clint, who stood his ground. He put his index finger an inch from Clint's face.

"Now, this *is* a threat, Mr. Adams," he said, "a threat and a promise. If you go anywhere near my wife, bring this up to her at any time, I will make you the sorriest man who ever lived. Do you understand me?"

"I understand you real well," Clint said. "Now let's make sure you understand me. If I discover that my friend was lynched I will not rest until I find every man who was in that lynch party and bring him to justice. Do you understand me?"

Kendall took a step back before answering.

"I think you were right, Adams."

"About what?"

"About me not wanting to sell you a horse after I heard why you were here," Kendall said. "I think you better get off my land, now."

"Just have your foreman bring my horse back around," Clint said, "and I'll be on my way."

"Just wait at the bottom of the steps," Kendall said. With that he turned and went into the house.

Clint went down the steps and waited, as instructed. When his horse was brought around it was not by the foreman, Walker, but by three other men—presumably ranch hands.

"This your horse?" one of them asked.

"It is."

"How do we know that?" the second man asked.

"Because I just told you."

"What if it ain't your horse and we give it to you," the third man said.

Clint studied all three men for a moment. Their intentions were not clear. They were unarmed, so apparently they hadn't been sent to kill him. If, however, they'd been sent to do him some harm it had been foolish of them to try to do it without guns when he obviously had his.

Clint dropped his hand down by his gun and said, "Let's get to it, boys."

SEVENTEEN

The three men exchanged a glance and then the first one—
the one holding the reins—asked, "Whataya mean?"

"I mean it doesn't take three of you to bring a man his
horse," Clint said. "You've obviously got something else
on your mind."

The first man looked behind him, while the other two
looked toward the house. It was unclear to Clint who had
given them their orders, the foreman or their boss, but they
were looking for guidance now.

"Let me guess," Clint said. "You're supposed to teach
me a lesson, and somebody told you that if you were unarmed you wouldn't have to worry about my gun. How am
I doing?"

The first man said, "You wouldn't shoot an unarmed
man."

"Why not?"

"Well . . . it ain't right," the second man said.

"Let me tell you what ain't right," Clint said. "It ain't
right for a man to be lynched without being given the
chance to prove his innocence. And it ain't right for a man
to be shot in the back while minding his own business."

"Who got shot in the back?" the third man asked.

"Somebody tried to shoot me in the back recently," Clint said, "and it's made me real testy. So to answer your question, yeah, I would shoot an unarmed man—or, to be more exact, three unarmed men if they meant to do me harm."

He let that sink in for a few seconds.

"So I'll say it again, boys," he went on. "Do what you came here to do."

The three men exchanged glances again, and then the first man held out the reins to Clint.

"Just came to bring you your horse, Mister."

Clint accepted the reins, walked the horse a distance away from the three men, then mounted up and rode off without another word.

After Clint left the foreman, Walker, came out of the barn and walked over to his three hands.

"What the hell happened here?" he demanded. "You were supposed to stomp some sense into him."

"He was gonna shoot us, boss," the first man said.

"Yeah," the second said, "guns or no guns, he wasn't gonna take no beating."

"He wouldn't have shot you," Walker said. "You're unarmed."

"Didn't make no never mind to him," the third man said.

"And he *is* the Gunsmith," the first man pointed out. "You said he was, and I wasn't takin' no chances. You can fire me if you want."

Walker glared at the three men and said, "I ain't gonna fire you."

All three men looked relieved.

"But if Mr. Kendall fires me I'll find the three of you and kick your asses," he finished. "Now get back to work."

He waited for them to get back to what they were supposed to be doing, and then went into the house.

• • •

Kendall listened to what he had to say and then sat back in his chair, drumming the fingers of his right hand on his desk.

"Nobody's getting fired, Walker."

"Thank you, sir."

"But I still want that man taught a lesson."

"It'll take more than three ranch hands to do it."

"Then get three men who will do it," Kendall said, "or as many as it will take. Understand?"

"Yes, sir."

"Now get out."

"Yes, sir."

Walker turned to leave and almost walked into his boss's wife, Jenny Kendall.

" 'scuse me, Miz Kendall."

As Walker left Jenny asked her husband, "What was that all about?"

"Just business, Jenny," Kendall said. "That's all."

"And who was that man you were talking to?"

"That was also business. What are you doing up? I thought the doctor put you to bed."

"I can't stay in bed forever, Allan," Jenny said. "I have to start living again, sometime."

Allan Kendall stared at his wife, wondering where the woman he married seven years ago had gone. She'd been beautiful then, and now she looked washed out and old. When Linda reached the age of thirteen she had suddenly blossomed and become the beautiful one of the two—and the one who most interested Allan Kendall. He still didn't know for sure if his wife knew about his nocturnal visits to his stepdaughter's bed. If she did she was still keeping quiet about it.

"Well," Kendall said, "that doesn't mean getting into my business, Jenny. I've got work to do."

"Was that man here about. . . . Linda?"

"I told you it was business!" Kendall said, exploding at his wife.

"Because we still don't know if that poor man Bates did it or not," she said. "We don't know—"

Kendall was around his desk and across the room before his wife knew what was happening. He grabbed her by the throat, cutting off the rest of her words.

"I told you never to mention that name, didn't I?" he asked. "Didn't I?" Flecks of spittle landed on her face as Jenny Kendall nodded her head jerkily.

He released her and she staggered back, grabbing her throat.

"Get out of here, Jenny. Go to your room and stay there."

"Dinner . . ." she said, in a small voice.

"I'll have a plate brought up to you," he said. "I don't want to sit across from your pinched face while I'm eating. Go on . . . get out!"

She turned and fled from the room. Kendall went back around behind his desk. He was going to get rid of her, but he had to wait a reasonable time after Linda's death. He also had to figure out the best way to do it, because divorce was just not an option. Not for him.

EIGHTEEN

Clint didn't think that Kendall or his foreman, Walker, were going to be happy with the outcome of the showdown with the three hands. Most likely—given the amount of money Kendall obviously had—the next set of men they sent would be armed, and much more experienced.

Clint rode back to town without incident. When he got there he realized how tense he had been in the saddle, expecting a bullet in the back the whole way. He left his horse at the livery and went to the saloon to celebrate still being alive with a beer.

This time he went to a saloon called Nell's. It was smaller than the first one he'd been to, but still larger than the one in French Creek. He went to the bar and ordered a beer from the young bartender.

"New in town?" the young man asked. He looked to be about twenty-five, although his cheeks were as smooth as a baby's.

"Got in today. You're a little young for this job, aren't you?"

"Nell believes in hiring the young."

"There really is a Nell?"

"Oh, yeah," the young man said. "She's the owner."

"How's the town feel about a woman owning and operating a saloon?" Clint asked.

"I don't think they care."

"What about girls? Did she hire them, too?"

"Nell hires the men," the bartender said, "her partner hires the girls."

"So the woman hires the men and the man hires the women?"

"No," the bartender said, "Nell's partner is a woman, too."

"Two women own this place?'

"That's right."

"How come there's only one name on it?"

"Nell's partner didn't want her name on it," the man said. "Besides, she's never here."

"Where is she?"

The young man shrugged and said, "I don't know. I think they own some other places."

"What's her name?"

"I don't know that, either," he said. "Maybe if you ask one of the girls they'll know, seein' as how she hired them."

"Thanks," Clint said. "If I get curious enough maybe I'll do that."

He looked around the place and saw that Nell's partner also believed in hiring the young. None of the three girls working the floor looked to be any older than the bartender.

"There she is," the bartender said, at that moment.

"Who?"

"Nell. Just came out of her office."

Clint looked and saw Nell, closing a door in the back wall.

"That's Nell?"

"That's her."

Nell was a big woman. Not a fat woman, necessarily, just big. She was wearing a dress like the saloon girls had on, showing lots of cleavage, only she had much more cleavage to show than any of them did. She had much more *skin* to show. She must have been five ten, but with her high heel shoes on she was over six feet. She was the type of woman who would not be to the taste of all men. Some men liked skinny women, some liked them small, but some men—like Clint—liked women, period.

Nell would be a challenge to most men, sort of like climbing a mountain just because it was there. Not that she was a mountain, she was just . . . a big woman.

As she moved around the room Clint saw that she was a big, *beautiful* woman, and she moved with all the grace and poise of a much more slender lady. She stopped at tables to talk to her customers, who looked her with a mixture of awe and interest. When she was finished making the rounds of the tables she came to the bar.

"How's it going tonight, Louie?" she asked the bartender.

"Just fine, Miss Nell."

"Louie," she said, stroking his chin, "how many times have I told you to call me Nell . . . just Nell, not Miss Nell."

"Sorry, Miss—I mean, Nell."

She laughed, looked at Clint and said, "He's a sweet boy, but so damn respectful all the time he makes me feel old."

"Hirc older bartenders," Clint suggested.

She turned to face him head on and he was impressed by her generous cleavage. Her big breasts were obviously firm, or being held up by a very strong foundation beneath her clothes. He understood some woman actually wore underwear made with whalebone, and he assumed that it would be large women who would do this. She also had the smoothest, most beautiful skin he'd ever seen and a peaches-and-cream complexion that had little to do with make-up.

"The only way for a bartender to get older," she said, "is for them to start young. I haven't seen you around here before."

"I just rode in today."

"Passin' through?"

"I'm here on business."

"What kind of business?"

"The personal kind."

"Wait a minute," she said, putting one hand on an ample hip, "are you that fella who was askin' questions today about Linda Kendall?"

"Word gets around," Clint said. Probably the newspaper editor, Henry Clarence. They'd spoken off the record, but that didn't mean the man wasn't going to *tell* anybody. Or maybe he had written about it. "Was that in the newspaper?"

"No," she said, "but I hear things."

"I'll bet."

"What's your interest in that?"

"I'd like to know who the man was who got hung.."

"Why?"

"I'm trying to locate a friend of mine and I can't. I'm hoping it wasn't him," he explained.

"Be a pure shame if it was," she said.

"Why's that?"

"If you been here a day, you probably already know."

"Because he was innocent?"

"And maybe the only person in the whole blame business who was," she said. "Look, I got to finish my rounds here, check up on the girls and the customers. We can talk later, if you like."

"I would like," he said. "Thanks."

"I'll be going back into my office in about an hour," she said. "Stick around until then?"

"Sure."

"Good," she said. "Louie, this fella is drinkin' on the house for as long as he's here."

"Okay . . . Nell."

"The door in the back of the room," she said. "Meet me there in an hour."

"I'll be there."

She nodded, turned and continued to move around the room.

"I don't know what you got, Mister," the bartender said, "but I never seen Nell make a friend that fast."

He didn't know exactly what he had, either, but he was going to find out in an hour.

NINETEEN

At the end of the hour he had only taken advantage of his situation once more to get a second beer and then he walked to the door of Nell's office. He had seen her go inside a little earlier, so he knocked.

"Come in!"

He opened the door and entered. The office was large, and decorated like the sitting room of a whorehouse, with gold and maroon brocade all over the place. Nell was seated behind a large desk, doing some paperwork, her cleavage threatening to spill out onto the desk top.

"Would you be a dear and pour us each a brandy. There's a small sidebar there against the wall. I just have to finish this paperwork."

"No problem."

He walked to the sidebar and poured two snifters of brandy from a crystal decanter. He walked to the desk and placed one there for her, then sat opposite her with his. He watched as she worked on her paperwork, saw that she was younger than he had first thought. The make-up fooled him, but she seemed to be in her early to mid-thirties. Maybe it was her attitude with the young bartender that had made her seem . . . more mature.

"I feel like I'm on display," she said, without looking up. "I can feel your eyes on me."

"It's your own fault," he said, "for being the kind of woman who attracts a man's eyes."

She looked up at him and smiled.

"It's the cleavage, isn't it?"

"If you'll pardon me for saying so, Nell," he answered, "it's the whole package, and you know it."

"You know," she said, putting aside her quill pen, "it's not every man who appreciates a big woman."

"It helps when the big woman is also beautiful."

She picked up her brandy snifter and sat back with it, regarding him with amusement etched on her face.

"I can see I'll have to be careful with you, Clint Adams."

"Why's that?"

"You're a man who knows how to talk to women."

"I'm sure you've heard it all before, Nell."

"Perhaps," she said, "but a woman always likes to hear it again."

"Well," he said, "maybe we can put this verbal sparring match aside for a moment while you tell me why you asked me back here."

She tapped the side of her glass with a crimson-colored nail and then said, "All right, but you have to promise that we'll come back to it."

"I promise."

"Good."

"Was it the newspaper editor, Henry Clarence, who told you why I was in town?" he asked.

"Yes," she said. "Henry came in for a drink earlier. We're friends because we both came to town at about the same time."

"Friends?"

"Just friends," she said, "although he's also a customer."

"Of the saloon?"

"Drinking and gambling is all I can offer Mr. Clarence," she said. "When he wants a woman it's usually something younger and . . . a little thinner."

"His loss."

"Definitely. Anyway, when he wrote his little editorial about the lynching I was one of the only people in town who felt the same way. That was why he came to me to tell me about you."

"And was there another reason?"

"I guess he thought maybe I could help you."

"In what way?"

"Maybe steering you in the right direction with your enquiries."

"And what direction would that be?"

"Away from the marshal, for one thing," Nell said.

"I figured out for myself that the marshal is a very politically minded man," Clint said.

"And his political future is firmly attached to Allan Kendall."

"That's no surprise."

"So you're not going to get much in the way of cooperation from the marshal," she said.

"How much do you know, Nell?"

"A lot of what goes on around town."

"The lynching?"

"What about it?"

"Did you know who the man was? His name?"

"I didn't," she said, "but I think I know where you can find out."

"Where?"

"It's my understanding that most of what that man wanted he got in Benson's Fork," she said. "I mean, supplies, food, whiskey . . . women. He got it all there."

"And how big is Benson's Fork?"

"A lot smaller than this town," she said, "and a lot bigger than French Creek."

"And how much do you know about French Creek?"

"What do you want to know?"

"I had the feeling I was being lied to the whole time I was there," he said. "The whole town seemed very uninterested in me, which I found odd. Towns are usually very curious about strangers, but not that one."

"French Creek is an odd little town," she said.

"You're telling me. There's also the bit about the Frenchman's Saloon and the Frenchman's House. Seems the owner just liked that name. And nobody ever sees him? This mysterious C. K. Healy?"

"What else?"

"Well, the sheriff there, Robbins? What's he about?"

"About the same as the marshal here."

"Well then, who's the law in Benson's Fork?"

"The marshal here enforces the law there," she said.

"Is there a deputy there?"

"Yes, but he reports to Marshal Dean."

"Also, somebody tried to kill me before I left French Creek. Tried to shoot me in the back and ended up killing my horse."

"There are all kinds of secrets hereabouts, Clint," she said. "And I mean, Sioux City, Benson's Fork and French Creek."

"Secrets worth killing for?"

"Oh, yes."

"For instance?"

"Oh," she said, "I don't know the secrets, exactly but . . . okay, for one thing your reclusive C. K. Healy?"

"Yes?"

"It's a woman."

"A woman? She owns the saloon and hotel in French Creek?"

"That's right."

"How do you know that?"

She smiled and said, "That's easy. She's my partner."

TWENTY

"Her name is Christine Healy," Nell said. "She's the money and I'm the brains."

"How does that work out?"

"Fine, as long as she stays in French Creek and I stay here."

"And why the 'Frenchman' names?"

"That was her idea, because of the name of the town." Nell shrugged. "I didn't argue. After all, I got to name this place."

"And do the two of you have a place in Benson's Fork?"

"No, not there. Christine—or C. K., as she prefers to be called—wanted to open a place in French Creek because it was so small and she wouldn't have to deal with a lot of people. She hates people."

"You're the opposite."

"That's right," she said. "I love being around people—especially men. Men fascinate me."

"Why?"

"Because they're very predictable," she said, "but every once in a while one comes along that surprises you. Those are the ones who make the whole kit-and-kaboodle of you fascinating."

"I see."

"You feel the same way about women, don't you?"

"I do, yeah," he said, nodding.

"I'll bet we have a lot in common."

"Like what?"

"Like wanting to find out who really killed that young girl—slut though she was—and also wanting to prove that poor man innocent."

"That's not what I want."

"It isn't?"

He shook his head.

"What do you want, then?"

"First I want to find out for sure if the lynched man was my friend," he said, "and second, if he was, I want to find the men who lynched him. Proving his innocence won't do anybody any good."

"He had no family?"

"No," Clint said, "and I don't know who else his friends were. So, as far as I know, it's just me who cares, and it's just me who is going to make the men who killed him pay."

"Vengeance."

"Yes."

"It's a male trait."

"Is it? Women don't yearn for vengeance?"

"Not the way men do," she said. "Women want to get even. That's a desire for justice, not vengeance."

"I see." He didn't necessarily agree, but why try to convince her? It wouldn't accomplish anything, and he wasn't there to have philosophical discussions about the differences between men and women.

"So in order to find out if the lynched man was my friend," he said, "you're saying I'd have to go to Benson's Fork."

"That's where I think your answer would be."

"Well, then," he said, "that's what I'll do."

"Tonight?" she asked.

"No," he said, "but first thing in the morning."

"Well then," she asked, tapping her teeth against the rim of the brandy snifter, "what did you have in mind for tonight?"

"I had no definite plans," he said. "Why? Do you have something in mind?"

"A long night of sex," she said, "and champagne, and getting to know one another . . . intimately."

"Wow," he said, "you're very direct."

"Only," she said, "when I see one of those very special men I was talking about before."

"The ones who make the whole kit-and-kaboodle of us interesting?"

She grinned and said, "That's the one."

TWENTY-ONE

Nell went into the saloon to tell the bartender that he was closing up that night, while Clint waited in her office. She had made him an offer he couldn't possibly refuse, and he did have to wait until morning to go to Benson's Fork. He couldn't think of a better way to spend the evening then checking under Nell's clothes to see if she wore whalebone underwear.

She came back into the office, took his hand and led him to another door. It led to her bedroom, which was conveniently located right behind her office.

"No living room?" he asked. "No kitchen?"

"These are the only two rooms I can't do without," she said, closing the door. She turned to face him, her back to it. "You're about to find out about this one."

She walked to him, then, eye-to-eye until she took off her shoes, and then she still wasn't that far off. She put her arms around his neck and pulled him close to kiss him. At the same time she pressed her body tightly to his and her breasts were like having two big pillows between them.

"I hope you like big women," she said, backing away from him.

"I love big women," he said, "and lots and lots of flesh."

"Well, you're in for a treat, then," she said, reaching behind her self to undo her dress, "because that's just what I've got."

She let the dress drop and stood before him in her underwear, which seemed to be made of a lot of lace, but no bone. Her opulant breasts jiggled as she bent to remove her stockings, and almost burst free. Finally, she stood and removed the underwear and she was right—she had a lot of flesh, and it was all smooth and pale and beautiful. And her scent—in the confines of her bedroom her scent filled his nostrils and it was a heady combination of perfume and the natural aroma of her skin.

She came to him, then, and began to unbutton his shirt. He reached behind her to fill his hands, cupping her majestic butt, which was firm and smooth. She removed his shirt and pressed her naked breasts against him. She was so hot he thought she was burning his skin, and her nipples were large and hard and pink.

He hadn't thought about her hair color at all, when he first saw her. Now it seemed to be a strawberry color, with the thick patch between her legs perhaps a shade or two darker.

He squeezed her butt and ran the middle finger of his right hand along the cleft between her cheeks. Her hands went down to his belt, encountered his gunbelt which he removed himself and set down very nearby. She unbuckled his belt, unbuttoned his pants and tugged them down to his ankles. He sat on the bed so she could remove his boots. Then she slid the trousers off and discarded them, and did the same to his underwear. Naked, his penis jutted up from his lap and she fell on it, stroking it, squeezing it, licking it, cooing to it and finally completely engulfing it in her hot mouth. Her breasts rested against his thighs as she suckled him, wetly, avidly, her head bobbing up and down, moaning as she sucked him to very near completion—and then let him slide free.

She straddled him, then, and lowered herself onto his ridged pole. She was wet, now, and the scent of her readiness added to the already intoxicating mix of smells in the room. She reached between them to hold his penis steady and then slid down, taking him inside of her. She lowered herself into his lap and her breasts were right there in front of him in all their majestic splendor. He'd read a story once about amazon women and Nell seemed the perfect incarnation of those female warriors.

He kissed her pale flesh, her neck, the slopes of her breasts, then lifted them to his mouth so he could suck her nipples. She kept her arms around his neck and rode him up and down, her head thrown back, biting her lower lip. He slid his hand between them so he could touch her where they were joined, wetting his fingers with her, stroking her until her eyes went wide and she moaned out loud as a wave of pleasure swept over her. She pushed him, then, so that he was lying on his back and began to ride him with more vigor. She bounced up and down on him so hard that the bed began to jump. He lifted his hips to meet every lunge, watched in fascination as her breasts jiggled and jumped in front of him. He ran his hands down her back to her hips, around to her butt, squeezing and pinching her flesh while she bounced her way to completion, her breathing coming in ragged intakes now, making it sound as if she were growling—and maybe she was.

When she was close he felt her body trembling and he turned her over—not without some difficulty, because she was a big woman and did not *want* to be turned over—so that she was on her back and he was on top.

He slid his arms beneath her thighs and lifted her legs so that her ankles were over his shoulders. He leaned into her then, and began to pound away at her, as hard or harder than she had been riding him.

"Yes, oh yes . . ." she babbled, glad now that he had flipped her into her back. His penis slid in and out of her slickly and she reached for him, pulled him down to her so she could kiss him, bite him, suck on him, urge him on with a flow of words in his ear which were hard for him to make out.

He slid his hands beneath her to cup her buttocks as he increased the speed and power of his lunges, the bed now not only jumping but banging into the wall . . . and then suddenly she made this high, keening sound and went off beneath him like a bucking bronco and it was all he could do to stay with her because she was so strong. He held on for dear life and finally exploded, emptying into her with a low bellow that he imagined could be heard right through the walls of the bedroom, the office and into the saloon . . . and beyond . . .

"You *do* like big women, don't you?" she asked. She was lying next to him on her back and you would think that breasts so big would flatten out when she was in that position, but they were also firm and they resisted the urge to flatten or slide or sag.

"I like this one," he said, running his hand over her belly, which was far from flat, and far from fat. It was solid, like the rest of her.

"Well, you're gonna have to prove it, sweetie," she said.

"I thought I just did."

"It's a long night," she said. "You're gonna have to prove it over and over . . . and over . . ."

TWENTY-TWO

Clint woke the next morning feeling pleasantly fatigued. As it turned out Nell was quite insatiable when it came to sex, but he was surprised to find that he was just as hungry and impossible to satisfy, that night. She was lying next to him on her side with no bedclothes covering her and he took a moment just to travel up and down the length of her with his eyes. Her skin was the creamiest he'd ever seen, as if no part of it had ever been exposed to the sun. He reached over and began to stroke her butt, just enjoying the way she felt beneath his hand.

"You're gonna get yourself into a lot of trouble that way," she said, without turning over.

"Trouble I can't handle?" he asked her.

"Oh, no," she said, looking at him over her rounded shoulder. "I don't think I can give you that kind of trouble. Not after last night. You proved you can handle me. That's rare in a man, believe me."

"Believe me," he said, "I do."

She rolled over, bringing those pink-tipped mounds of flesh into view, and asked, "Think you could handle me in the morning?"

"I think I could give it my best try . . ."

She started to roll over but he pushed her onto her back and kissed her, sliding his hand down over her soft belly into the hair between her legs. He found her and fingered her until she was good and wet. He kissed and nibbled her nipples, then blazed a wet trail down her body until his face was nestled in that fragrant forest and his tongue was avidly tasting her, sliding in and out of her, gliding up and down, causing her whole body to go as tense as a guitar string. He used his arms and elbows to pin her to the bed and then, just using his tongue and his lips he pulled that string tighter, and tighter and tighter until . . .

Snap!

"Whew!" she said, lying on her back next to him. "Damn, but you could kill a woman that way. Where did you learn to do that with your tongue?"

"It's a natural talent."

"Whoo-wee, it sure is!" she said, still trying to catch her breath. "You know, I wouldn't be able to move for a while if it wasn't for one thing."

"What's that?"

"I'm starving."

"I'm kind of hungry, too."

"Let's get dressed," she said, "and I'll buy you a big breakfast like none you've ever had before."

"You get that someplace special in town?"

"Oh, yeah," she said, "someplace special, all right—here!"

"Here" meant right out in the saloon. When they came out through the office door he could already smell something cooking.

"I have my breakfast prepared here every day," she said. "It's the benefit of owning your own place."

His friend Rick Hartman did the same thing in Labyrinth, Texas, in his saloon called Rick's Place. When Clint was in town he sometimes joined him for breakfast. This was the same kind of arrangement—except most nights he had spent with his friend had been spent drinking, not doing what he and Nell had done all night . . .

They seated themselves at what he assumed was Nell's table and then the young bartender appeared carrying a tray of food. Apparently, he had other talents besides tending bar.

He put the food on the table and Clint was looking at flapjacks, thick slabs of ham, a mess of scrambled eggs, and a basket of hot biscuits.

"You eat like this every day?" he asked.

"No," she said, "not quite. I gave Louie special instructions last night before we went to my room."

"You were pretty sure I'd stay the night."

"I was sure once I got you into my bed," she said, "I could keep you there."

He had gotten dressed but she had simply put on a dressing down, belted around her waist, and it was gaping so that he—and Louie—could see most of her breasts. Louie took a good look before heading back to the kitchen.

"Poor Louie," she said.

"Why poor?"

"He wants to be where you were all night."

"You mean he never has been?"

"God, no," she said, "He's so young. I hire young men, I don't sleep with them. I've told him over and over that any of the others would have him in a minute, but he's not interested in girls his own age."

"How could they compare to you?" he asked.

"True," she said, 'but why tease him so much?"

She rearranged her dressing down so that it covered some of her cleavage, but there was still plenty to go around.

"Let's eat," she said. "You want to head to Benson's Fork today, don't you?"

"I do," he said. "Are you looking to get me out of here so quick?"

"No," she said, smiling and smearing a biscuit with some jam. "I figure the faster you get there, the faster you'll get back and we can have us another night like we had last night. We need to have at least one more before you're on your way. I figure two nights like that should hold me for a while after you're gone."

"Maybe my business will keep me here even longer."

"Well, I'm not a foolish woman, Clint," she said. "I know that if I count on less and get more I'll feel lucky, and if I count on less and get it, I won't be disappointed."

"That's a good philosophy to live by."

"It is, except for one thing."

"What's that?"

"Usually, when I count on less," she said, "I get even less than that."

TWENTY-THREE

Clint had not yet had time to look for a horse so he intended to take the rented mare from the livery and head for Benson's Fork. He started for the livery but as soon as he stepped out of the hotel he was fronted by the marshal.

"A word with you, Adams?" Marshal Dean asked.

"Sure, Marshal," he said. "What can I do for you?"

Dean joined him on the boardwalk in front of the saloon.

"I was on my way over to the hotel to talk to you, but then I saw you come out of here," the lawman said. "A little early for Nell to be open, isn't it?"

"She's not open," Clint said. "I was just having breakfast with her."

Dean looked surprised, and not pleased.

"You and Nell old friends?"

"We only met last night," Clint said, "but we're friends now."

That made Dean frown, but then he got to the matter at hand—which didn't surprise Clint, at all.

"I understand you paid Mr. Kendall a visit."

"I did."

"What for?"

97

"Just to ask a few questions."

"He's real upset about those questions," Kendall said. "He doesn't want you upsetting his wife."

"I didn't talk to his wife."

"He wants to head you off before you do."

"So he sent you?" Clint asked. "I thought you worked for the town, Marshal, not for one man."

Dean smiled at the attempt to get his goat.

"Mr. Dean is a member of this community, Adams," he said. "What upsets any member of this community upsets me."

"I see," Clint said. "Well, you tell Mr. Kendall that I don't intend to upset his wife. I do, however, intend to find out who killed his daughter."

"Are you saying you don't think we already know that?"

"You don't know anything, Marshal," Clint said. "You don't know who the lynched man was, or what he did. I intend to find out."

"Are you a detective, now?"

"No," Clint said, "I'm just somebody who's going to keep asking questions until I get the right answers."

"Don't run afoul of the law, Adams," Dean said. "That would not be a good idea."

"Duly noted, Marshal," Clint said. "I've been warned. Now, if you'll excuse me, I've got things to do."

"I'm going to be watching you, Adams."

"That's good, Marshal," Clint said, "because that'll allow me to keep an eye on you at the same time."

Dean looked surprised.

"And why would you want to keep an eye on me?" he asked.

"Because you're the kind of lawman I don't like, Marshal."

"And what kind is that?"

"The politically motivated kind," Clint answered. "The

kind who thinks his badge is a stepping stone to something better. The kind who is more concerned with his own future than with what's best for the law."

"Looking out for your future has never been a bad thing," Dean said.

"Well," Clint said, "I guess we disagree on that, Marshal. Looking out for your future, that's personal, and upholding the law, that's business. I've never thought that mixing your personal life with your business was a very good idea."

"I understand that you wore a badge once, Adams," Dean said, "but times have changed since then."

"The law's the law, Marshal," Clint said. "It doesn't change. Only the people assigned to uphold it change."

"I'm not here to debate you, Adams," Dean said, "just to deliver a—just to tell you how it is."

He'd almost said he was there to "deliver a message." That would have been the truest thing he'd said since Clint had met him.

"Consider it delivered, Marshal," Clint said. "Now excuse me, but I've got a lot of things to do today."

He pushed past the lawman and headed for the livery.

TWENTY-FOUR

When Clint got to the livery there was nobody there. He went inside to get the horse but it wasn't there, either. He went outside to look in the corral, but the mare wasn't there, either. Now he went looking for the liveryman, and found him out in back of the building.

"Hey!"

The man turned and looked at him. He had watery eyes and a weak chin and could have been forty or fifty.

"What happened to my mare?"

"Huh?"

"The mare I rode in on," Clint said. "That's a rented horse. I'm responsible for it. Where is it?"

"I dunno."

"You put her in a stall yesterday when I rode in, didn't you?"

"Uh-huh."

"Well, she isn't in there now," Clint said. "Where is she?"

"I—I dunno."

The man's eyes were shifty and he was nervous. He knew, all right, but he was afraid to tell. Whatever or who-

101

ever he was afraid of Clint was going to have to make him more afraid of *him* at that moment.

"Look friend," he said, moving closer to the man, "I'm a little short on patience right now. I need my horse and it isn't around. Now you tell me what happened to it or this town is going to have to find somebody else to do your job."

He moved a step closer and the man broke.

"Mister, honest, I only did what I was told," he blubbered. "I—I ain't done nothin' but look the other way."

"While somebody took my horse?"

"Y-yeah."

"Who?"

"I—I can't say . . . they'd hurt me . . ."

"I'll hurt you right now if you don't say," Clint said. "You've got to be more afraid of me, man, because I'm right here."

The man held both hands up in front of his face and said, "I-it was a couple of guys from the Kendall ranch. T-they walked in, give me a dollar and told me if I knew what was good for me I'd go get a drink."

"And?"

"And I went!"

"And when you came back?"

"I noticed your horse was gone."

How had they known which horse to take? Sure, if they were from the Kendall ranch they had seen him on the horse earlier in the day.

"Mister," the liveryman said, "it wasn't the dollar. I was . . . I was real scared . . ."

Suddenly, Clint felt terrible for scaring the man again.

"Forget it," Clint said. "I need a horse."

"I can't—"

Clint got mad and forgot about feeling terrible.

"I gave you my horse and you lost it," he said. "Now I

need one to ride to Benson's Fork and back. I'll return it
tonight or tomorrow—that is, unless somebody steals it."

"Mister—"

"You've got plenty of horses, friend," Clint said. "If anyone asks tell them I gave you a dollar and told you to go
get a drink."

Finally, the man relented.

"Your saddle is still inside," he said. "Pick any horse out
of the corral."

"Thank you," Clint said, sarcastically.

Clint turned and went back inside the livery. He hadn't
noticed but his saddle *was* still there. He lugged it out to
the corral and then looked over the horses that were there.
They weren't a great lot but he picked out a four- or five-
year-old gelding and went into the corral to get it. They
were all stock that had been broken, so he was able to walk
up to it and lead it to the gate. First he put a bridle in it,
then his blanket and saddle. While he was pulling the cinch
tight he became aware that someone had come walking up
to the corral and was watching him over the gate.

When he finished with the saddle he looked and saw
three men watching him. Through the gate he could see
that they were all wearing handguns.

These were definitely not ranch hands.

TWENTY-FIVE

"Well, lookee here, boys," the first man said. "Looks like we caught ourselves a horse thief."

"Why would a fella go and do somethin' like that?" the second man asked. "Makes a body wonder, don't it?"

"Unless," the third man said, "somebody stole his horse and he thinks he's entitled to steal another one."

"That what it is, Mister?" the first man asked. "You think you're entitled to steal a horse?"

"Mine was stolen while inside the livery stable," Clint said. "The liveryman feels responsible, and he's replacing it. Why don't you go and ask him, yourselves?"

The second and third man looked directly at the first, which right away determined the pecking order here, for Clint. The first man, however, was apparently not that used to making decisions, because he looked perplexed, for the moment.

"So why don't the three of you just move away from the gate and I'll be on my way," Clint added, and started toward the gate.

Marshal John Dean stood his ground and watched as Clint Adams walked away from him. He prided himself on the fact that he was not completely in the pocket of Allan Kendall, but he also did not want to get on the wrong side of the man. Surely, just delivering a message on the man's behalf did not compromise him as a lawman. After all, he needed the backing of someone like Allan Kendall if he was going to move into the political arena.

But the murder of the Kendall girl still worried him. With no clear-cut evidence that the man who had been hung was actually guilty would this come back and haunt him sometime in the future when he was running for office? Did he want some old case like this to interfere with his entire political future?

He had some quick decisions to make.

Would it be more politically advantageous to him to help Clint Adams with his inquiries and find out the truth?

Or should he simply close his eyes to the lynching and hope that this all just went away?

What if the truth was that Allan Kendall himself was somehow involved in the death of his own stepdaughter, and people realize he'd done nothing about it?

He stood there, shaking his head, suddenly unsure of even what direction to walk in.

Still unsure of what to do, the three men found themselves backing away from the gate as Clint opened it and walked through. He wondered if he was going to be able to get mounted before they could recover—but that wasn't to be.

"Now, wait a minute," the first man said. "You can't just mount up and ride out of here."

"Why not?" Clint asked.

"Well . . . it ain't right, is why."

"Okay," Clint said. He tossed the reins over the top of the corral and turned to face the three men. "Let's get this over with."

"W-whataya mean?" the first man asked.

"Come on, you were obviously sent over here to do a job," Clint said. "What was it?"

Nobody answered.

"To scare me?"

Blank stares.

"To hurt me?"

The second and third man looked helplessly to the first, again.

"To kill me?"

No answer.

"Why don't we just do this?" Clint said. "If you were sent to scare me, you haven't. If you were sent to hurt me, that's not going to happen. If you were sent to kill me . . . well then, have at it and let's get it done."

"But . . . there's three of us," the third man said.

"I don't care how many of you there are," Clint said. "If even one of you touches his gun, I'll kill all three."

The three men looked puzzled. How could one man facing three guns talk that way?

"This ain't right, Billy," the third man said to the first.

"Look at him," the second man said. "He's *willin'* to face all three of us."

"He's either crazy . . ." the third man said.

". . . or he's that good," the second man said.

"Ah," Billy said, "nobody's that good."

"I'm sorry, Billy," the third man said, "I ain't been paid enough to find out for sure."

"Me neither," the second man said, and the two of them backed away, and then walked away.

"What about you, Billy?" Clint asked. "You being paid enough to find out for sure . . . on your own?"

Billy stared at Clint for a few moments, his right arm cocked to go for his gun, and then suddenly he relaxed it and eased his hand away.

"Naw," he said, "naw, I ain't."

He turned and walked away.

Clint retrieved the reins from the top of the corral, mounted up and rode out of Sioux City, heading for Benson's Fork.

TWENTY-SIX

The description of Benson's Fork that Clint had received had been accurate. Certainly not the size of Sioux City, but considerably larger than French Creek. And he had not come to a fork in the road anywhere between there and Sioux City—not that it mattered.

He rode in and was relieved to find that he became the object of immediate curiosity. People working stopped to look at him, and others who were just walking did the same. This was a far cry from the treatment he'd received in French Creek, and he still did not know why that was. And he wasn't sure he wanted to go back there to find out.

He didn't ride to the livery. It had taken him two hours to ride there, and he was hoping to return to Sioux City the same day. He found the office of the deputy marshal and dismounted there, tying off the gelding and mounting the boardwalk. He tried the door but found it locked. He turned and looked up and down the street. There was activity in front of some of the stores, but at that moment no one was approaching him from either direction.

He had not seen any telegraph wires while riding in, so he doubted that Marshal Dean would have been able to get word to the deputy that he was coming to town. Maybe the man was making rounds, or having a meal.

Clint chose the closest business to the office, which was a hardware store, and walked over to it. He went inside and drew the attention not only of the clerk but of the two men who were customers.

"Any of you gents know where the deputy went?"

"Deputy?"

"Yes, the deputy marshal?"

The three of them exchanged a glance, and then the two customers went back to what they were doing. The clerk, a balding man in his fifties, came around the counter and approached Clint.

"Mister, we ain't had a deputy here in months. Last one we had up and quit and left town."

"What do you do for law problems?"

"We usually send somebody for the marshal in Sioux City. Ain't but two hours away—less on a fast horse."

"I know," Clint said, "I just came from there."

"You left there to come here?" the man asked, surprised. "Usually works the other way around."

For some reason Marshal Dean had sent him on a wild goose chase to talk to the deputy who didn't exist, but maybe it didn't have to end up that way.

"Do you know a man named Artemus Bates?"

"Bates?" the man said. "Sure do. Lives not too far from here on a little place. Got some horses, I think."

Clint's heart started to beat faster. Finally, someone who knew who he was talking about.

"How do you know him?"

"He comes in here a couple of times a month to pick up what he needs out there. Says he don't like Sioux City. Too big, too busy he says, and the whiskey is watered down." The man laughed. "He says the women, too."

"When's the last time you saw him?"

The man scratched his nose while he thought.

"I believe he was in here last month," he said. "Might even have been three weeks. I expect he'll be ridin' in again, real soon. You a friend of his?"

"I am," Clint said. "I've been looking for him. I thought he lived closer to French Creek."

"Nope," the man said, "closer to here."

"Can you tell me exactly where his place is?"

"Sure," the man said, and as he gave Clint directions to Artemus Bates's house Clint's heart sank lower and lower.

"Think you can find it?" the man asked, when he was done.

"I think I already did," Clint said. It was the place he'd found that had been ransacked.

"Wasn't Artie there?"

"Mister, what's your name?"

"Art Kaline."

"Mr. Kaline, what do you know about the murder of a little girl from Sioux City?"

"Good Lord!" Kaline said, when Clint was finished. "They hung Artie?"

"That's the way it seems," Clint said. "I haven't seen a body, but it's starting to look that way."

"It can't be," Kaline said.

"Can you think of someplace else he might be?"

"He's goes fishin' sometimes, a little fishin' hole near here, but he wouldn't be there for so long."

"Does he have a woman he'd go see?"

"Only women he goes to see he pays for," Kaline said. "He says the only way to get a woman to keep treatin' you right is to pay her."

"Mr. Kaline, was it a coincidence that I stopped in here and you know who he was and are friends with him?"

"Hell, no," Kaline said. "Go to the General Store or the

Feed and Grain. They know him, too, and they're friends with him."

"Can you tell me why nobody in French Creek or Sioux City knows who he is?" Clint asked.

"I told you," Kaline said, "he only comes here."

"You have a whorehouse?"

"Got one with three girls in it. We got two saloons, and couple of cafes. Artie said we had everything he needed right here."

"Word never got back here about the lynching?"

"We heard somethin' about it," Kaline said, "but we never thought it was Artie they hung."

"Lynched," Clint said. "If you knew Artie—and it sounds like you knew him even better than me—you know he'd never do anything like that to a young girl."

"Oh, hell, I know that," Kaline said, "and so does everybody in this town. He couldn'ta done what they say. Maybe you're wrong, Mister. Maybe it wasn't Artie they hung, at all."

"Believe me, Mr. Kaline," Clint said. "I'd like nothing better than to see him come riding down the street right now, or to find him with one of the three whores you mentioned."

"Maybe one of the others know where he is," Kaline said. "Come on."

"What about your store?"

"I'll close up," Kaline said. "Let me get these two customers out of here."

He took care of whatever purchase they were making and then turned the sign on the door from open to closed.

"It's nice of you to do this," Clint said.

"Hell, Artie's life is worth more than me sellin' another hammer or ten-penny nail. Come on, let's go see if anybody's seen him."

TWENTY-SEVEN

Kaline took him to the general store, where they talked to a man named Sven Lindstrom. Lindstrom knew who Artie Bates was and liked him, but he hadn't seen him in about three weeks.

At the Feed & Grain it was a man named Anderson who said the same thing. He hadn't seen Bates in three weeks, and if he wasn't at his house he didn't know where to look for him.

They went to the whorehouse and talked to the three girls there. Actually, one was a girl, about eighteen or nineteen. Her name was Alice. Another, who called herself Pepper, was in her late thirties and going to fat. The third was a tall, slender brunette named Diane who, although she was past forty, looked better than Pepper, who was younger. Probably had something to do with the fact that she was thin, Clint thought. Anyway, none of the three women had seen Bates in three weeks, and he didn't prefer one woman over the other. They claimed that every time he came he simply alternated. He always remembered who he had been with the last time, and who he was going to be with next time.

Kaline took Clint to several other places with the same results, and they ended up in one of Benson Fork's two saloons, called simply No. 7.

"If there's only two in town," Clint asked, over a beer, "why is it called Number seven?"

"Who knows?" Kaline asked.

They sat at a table in the saloon, which had only a few customers at that time of the afternoon.

"I don't get it," Clint said.

"What?"

"How could Artie be so well known here and so utterly unknown in two other towns near here?"

"Maybe," Kaline said, "if he'd spent more time in Sioux City they wouldn't have lynched him. They would have known him better, and known he couldn't have done such a thing."

"They needed to lynch somebody," Clint said.

"Why?"

"So nobody would be looking for the real killer."

"And why Artie?"

"It was *because* he wasn't known in town," Clint said, "because he was a stranger, with no family."

"Nobody to miss him," Kaline said.

"If he's stopped coming here to do his shopping what would you have thought?" Clint asked.

"Probably that he'd moved on."

"Exactly."

"So what they didn't count on," Kaline said, "what they couldn't count on . . ."

". . . was me," Clint said. "Me coming up here to look for him. They made one try to kill me, and a couple to intimidate me."

"What will they try next?" Kaline asked.

"They'll have to send someone next time who won't be intimidated," Clint said, "and who won't back down."

"A professional killer," Kaline said.

"Yes," Clint said, "and with the Kendall money he'll be the best they can possibly buy."

"Why don't you just leave?" Kaline asked. "Forget about the whole thing? Why risk your life?"

"Because I need to know for sure if the lynched man was Artemus Bates," Clint said. "I can't leave here until I do."

"I get the feeling that by trying to make you leave," Kaline said, "they're just succeeding in making you stay."

"Are you saying I'm stubborn?"

"I'm saying you're stubborn."

"Well," Clint said, "I guess somebody has to be."

Kaline raised his beer mug and said, "Here's to finding Artie Bates alive."

"I'll drink to that," Clint said.

But both men knew there was little or no chance of that.

TWENTY-EIGHT

Allan Kendall was not a happy man.

"This is the second time you've sent men who couldn't do the job, Walker," he said. "What's the problem?"

"Good guns are hard to come by, sir," Walker said. "They're real expensive."

"Are you trying to save me money, Walker?" Kendall asked. "Is that it? Because I've got plenty, you know. I don't need you to try and save me money. I need you to hire men who can get the job done."

"Yes, sir," Walker said. "I'll do that."

"I want them here by the time Adams gets back from Benson's Fork."

"That might be tonight," Walker said. "It's not that long a ride, and there's not much there for him to find out."

"All right," Kendall said. "Get them here, that's the important thing. I'll give you two days to get this done, Walker."

"That's all I'll need, sir," Walker said. "I guarantee it."

"That's good," Kendall said, "because I guarantee if you don't get it done, in three days you won't have a job!"

• • •

There wasn't much more to do in Benson's Fork. Granted, everyone here seemed to know Artie Bates, but there was nothing to help Clint in his effort to identify the lynched man. He decided that there was no way you could lynch a man and not know his name, first. Somebody—probably someone in the actual lynch party—knew who the man was. Clint had to take a new route now. He had to try to identify the men who were in the lynch party. When he did that, he was sure one of them would be able to tell him for sure whether or not the lynched man was Artie Bates.

"Sorry we couldn't be more help," Kaline said, as Clint mounted his borrowed gelding in front of the man's store.

"You did what you could," Clint said. "At least I found some people who knew Artie. I was starting to think I was crazy and that he didn't exist."

"What's your next step?"

Clint told Kaline what he was thinking about identifying the members of the lynch party.

"Does sound like your best bet," Kaline said, "but you better be careful. It doesn't sound like you have any help in Sioux City."

"There are a couple of people there who are on my side," Clint said, "but they wouldn't be much help if it came to gunplay, that's for sure."

"Well, I wouldn't, either," Kaline said, "or I'd try to help."

"You've done enough," Clint said. He reached down to shake the man's hand. "All my answers now are in Sioux City, I think. I'll just get back there and not leave town without them."

"Good luck," Kaline said.

Clint wheeled the gelding around and pointed it back to Sioux City.

• • •

Walker realized that his boss was right. He had been trying not to spend much money, but now he had free rein to spend whatever it took. When he got back to town he went to the telegraph office and sent out three messages. If only one was received, he knew all three men would respond. These were men who not only wore guns, but knew how to use them, and who didn't intimidate. In fact, when they found out that their target was the Gunsmith that would just make them even more eager.

He sent the telegrams then stepped outside and came face to face with Marshal John Dean, the lawman Kendall had in his pocket.

"Afternoon, Marshal."

Dean hated Kendall's foreman, the man they all called Walker. He always looked at the lawman with amusement in his eyes, like he found something funny about him and his badge.

"Running errands, Walker?" Dean asked.

"Taking care of some business, Marshal," Walker said. "Doing my job, which is somethin' we should all be doin'."

"I do my job," Dean said.

"Sure you do, Marshal," Walker said, "sure you do. I didn't say that you didn't. By the way, seen Clint Adams around lately?"

"He rode out this morning," Dean said, "headed in the direction of Benson's Fork."

"Wonder if he stopped there or just kept goin'," Walker said.

"Oh, he'll stop there," Dean said, "and he'll be back here, probably tonight."

"What makes you say that?"

"Because he's got the bit in his teeth now," Dean said, "and he's not going to let loose until he gets the answers he's looking for."

"Maybe," Walker said, "or maybe he'll find that he bit off more than he could chew."

"What's that mean?"

"Nothin'," Walker said. "Just talkin', Marshal, that's all . . . just talkin'. You take care, now."

Walker strode away, his demeanor annoying to Marshal Dean, who felt the man was still laughing at him. Dean wouldn't have minded at all if Walker managed to get in Clint Adams's way.

He wondered what errand Walker had been on for his boss, Kendall. He watched the man's retreating back until he was out of sight and then went into the telegraph office to see what he could find out.

TWENTY-NINE

By the time Clint returned to Sioux City it was getting dark. It occurred to him that some sort of ambush might have been set up at the livery and he approached carefully, but it turned out not to be the case. He was being extra cautious because he had nobody watching his back here. It was a bad situation to be in a town the size of Sioux City, not know exactly who your enemies were, and have no friends to back you up.

The liveryman accepted the horse without comment, except to say, "I'll keep him available for ya."

"Let me know if the gray mare turns up," Clint said. "I'd still like to be able to return it to the man I rented it from."

"Yes, sir."

He left the livery and walked back through town to his hotel. He wondered if he should send out some telegrams, maybe get some help, but the people he would have sent them to would be at least two or three days away, maybe more. None of the people he would trust to watch his back—Wyatt Earp, Bat Masterson, Luke Short—would be in Minnesota for any reason. And he had a feeling this whole thing was going to come to a head before anyone would be able to get there. No, he was going to have to see this thing through to the end himself.

He had some questions, and he thought it was more likely that the newspaper editor, Clarence, would have the answers than Nell would. He detoured away from his hotel to the newspaper office, hoping to find the man working late, but the place was locked up and there were no lights inside. Since he didn't know where the man lived he went back to his original plan and headed for the hotel to freshen up before going to the saloon.

As he entered Nell's nobody looked at him, it was that busy. The gaming tables were going full bore, all the tables were taken and there was barely space at the bar. The three young girls were working very hard on the floor, entertaining the men who were not gambling. At that moment, Nell was nowhere to be seen and her table was the only empty table in the place.

He walked to the bar and managed to elbow himself a space. Louie, the bartender, spotted him and came over.

"You still drinkin' on the house?" he asked.

"No," Clint said, "I'll pay. I'll start with a beer."

"Comin' up."

Louie went down the bar and returned with Clint's beer, then quickly had to go and serve someone else.

Clint turned with his beer in hand and looked the room over. He thought he might spot the newspaperman, Henry Clarence, there but did not. He did, however, see the three hands who had braced him at the Kendall place, and at another table—a blackjack table—he saw the foreman, Walker. He walked over so he could see the man's hand as he played. His game was steady, but cautious. Clint had never liked blackjack that much. He felt the returns—two and a half to one on Blackjack—were too meager for the time spent, considering what you could win in a single hand of poker for the same stakes.

"Gonna try my tables?" Nell asked. Coming up from behind him.

"Not blackjack," Clint said. "Do you run a house poker game?"

She pressed her breasts into his side and said, "No, but I can set up a private game, if you like."

"The only private game I'm interested in is with you, Nell," he said, which pleased her.

Clint was still watching Walker's game while they talked. The man had just lost two hands in a row with a nineteen and a twenty, and wasn't taking it well. He was glaring at the dealer, who managed to pull twenty and then make blackjack—just enough to beat Walker.

"How did your day in Benson's Fork go?"

He glanced at her and his gaze was immediately attracted to her deep cleavage. He pulled his eyes away and looked back at the blackjack table. Walker was slamming his cards down. Clint couldn't see what he had, but apparently he'd been beaten again by the dealer.

"Well, at least they knew who Artie Bates was," Clint said, "but nobody has seen him in about three weeks."

"So it still could have been him."

"Possibly."

"What are you thinking?"

He hesitated, then said, "I'm pretty sure it was him. One of the men in Benson's Fork told me where Artie lived. It was the house I found ransacked, with the door kicked in."

"I'm sorry," she said. "What are you going to do next?"

"Find the men who were in the lynch party."

"That won't be easy."

"Maybe not," Clint said. "It's been my experience, though, that when you get a group of men together for something like that, one of them will usually brag about it.

I just have to find that one man. He'll lead me to the rest."

"And then what?"

He sipped his beer and said, "And then they'll pay for what they did. Do you have some security in this place?"

"I usually rely on the marshal for that," Nell said, "or the bartender. Why?"

"Your blackjack dealer is straight, isn't he?"

"As far as I know. Why?"

"He's been beating the foreman of the Kendall ranch's brains in for the past five or six hands."

"Walker?"

"Is he a regular?"

"He is."

"Does he win?"

"Always loses."

"And he's a bad loser, isn't he?"

"Oh, yes."

"Well, he's about to explode, I think."

"Maybe I can keep him from—" she said, but it was too late.

"Goddamnit!" Walker shouted, hopping off the stool he was sitting at. "You're cheatin'!"

"No, I'm not, sir," the dealer said, politely.

"Then how can you keep beating me by one?" Walker demanded. "I get eighteen you get nineteen, I get nineteen you get twenty, I get twenty and you get blackjack. Hell, I stood with thirteen once and you got fourteen! You mean to tell me you ain't cheatin' me?"

"No, sir, I'm not," the man said.

"What do you call it, then?"

"A really bad run of luck, sir," the dealer said.

"Walker," Nell said, coming alongside the man. "You know how luck runs. Bad for a while, then good. Just ride it out."

"I ain't got enough money to ride it out," Walker complained. "Your dealer is cheatin' me, Nell."

"He's not."

"You just don't see it," Walker said to her. "Well, I'll make him admit it."

And the foreman of the Kendall ranch went for his gun.

THIRTY

Clint stepped forward quickly as the dealer backed up a step and brought his hand up in front of his face, as if that would ward off a bullet. Nell was also bringing her hands up, but Clint thought she was going to make a lunge for Walker. He pushed her aside and got his left hand on Walker's hand as the man grabbed his gun. He held the gun in the holster that way, and Walker could not get it out.

"What the hell—" he said, turned his head and saw Clint. "Let go of my hand!" he demanded.

"Ease up, Walker," Clint said. "Don't make me take my gun out."

Walker suddenly realized who Clint was and what was happening. He didn't want to get involved in gunplay with the Gunsmith. Suddenly, he relaxed his arm. Clint took his hand away and Walker dropped his hand from his gun.

"Settle down," Clint said. "You're having a run of bad luck. The dealer is straight. I've been watching him."

"Yeah," Walker said, "yeah, a run of bad luck. Can happen to anybody, right?"

"Right."

"Even you, right?" Walker asked.

Clint thought they were suddenly not talking about blackjack.

"That's right," he said, "even me."

Walker left on his own, scowling and stuffing what was left of his money into his pockets.

"Thank you," the dealer said to Clint. He was a young man, like the bartender, and good looking. Clint found it hard to believe that Nell was not sleeping with any of the young men she'd hired.

"Just about knocked me down," Nell said, "but thanks for the help."

"I saw you," Clint said. "You were going to go for him."

"I got to protect my boys."

"You could have got yourself killed."

"I didn't think about that until after."

Clint looked around, realizing he had lost his beer. It was on the floor, the mug shattered. He didn't realize he had dropped it.

"I'll have someone clean that up," she assured him, taking his arm. "Come on to the bar. The house owes you a drink."

They walked to the bar together and now that he was in Nell's company a big spot opened up for them.

"Louie, a beer for Mr. Adams."

"Yes, Ma'am."

"And one for me."

Louie put two beers on the bar.

"What did Walker mean about your luck being bad?" she asked.

"I guess he meant it was about to turn bad."

"That's only because he doesn't know about last night."

"I'll drink to last night," Clint said, and they clinked mugs.

•   •   •

Walker staggered angrily to his horse when he left the saloon. He was drunker than he'd thought and on top of that
he was angry not only at Clint Adams, but at himself, as
well. He always told himself he wasn't going to let his
temper get the better of him when he gambled, but it never
happened that way. Now he'd gone and made a fool of
himself, and Adams was a big part of that.

Big man with a gun, he thought, mounting up. In a day
or two he wouldn't be so big.

The rest of the night went without incident, and about an
hour before closing the newspaperman, Henry Clarence,
came in, got himself a beer and corralled one of the girls
from the floor. He put his arm around her and looked like
he was going to settle in for the night with her.

"Must have had another fight with his wife," Nell said.

"He's married?"

"Sort of," Nell said. "See, his wife has some money and
it's her who owns the newspaper."

"Seems to be a lot of women in this town owning businesses.

"We know how to run them," she said.

"So what's the story? Are they always fighting?"

"Not always," Nell said, "just two or three times a day.
Whenever they have a big one he comes in here and spends
the night with one of my girls."

"Never with the boss?"

She made a face and said, "I have better taste than to
sleep with a man who can be whipped by a woman."

"I was looking for him earlier."

"What for?"

"I need some information."

"And you'd go to him before me?"

"He's the newspaperman," Clint said. "News and information are his business."

"What do you need information about?"

"Likely members of a lynch party."

"Hmph," she said, indignantly, "well, you go and see what you can find out from him, and then come to me and see if I'll give you any information."

"Nell—"

"No, no," she said, "that's all right. You go and try the *man* first. I'll be waiting."

THIRTY-ONE

Clint approached Henry Clarence, who was on his second beer and second girl. Apparently, he hadn't picked the girl he wanted, yet.

"Mr. Clarence."

Clarence looked at him.

"Could I have a word with you?"

"Don't go too far, dear," Clarence said to the girl, who sashayed off. "Buy you a beer?"

"No, thanks," Clint said. "I just wanted to ask you a few questions."

"Why should I answer them?"

"Well . . . you were the one who wanted me to help, remember?"

"Yes," Clarence said, "and I remember you were the one who wouldn't give me an interview, remember?"

"I don't do interviews."

"Well," Clarence said, "maybe I don't answer questions."

"You're changing your tune, then?" Clint asked. "You don't want to know the truth?"

Clarence stared at him, then put his beer mug down.

"I'm sorry," he said, passing a hand over his forehead.

"I had a fight with my wife tonight. It's made me . . . disagreeable."

"I understand?"

"Do you?" the man asked. "Do you understand why people get married? Jesus, I don't. Oh, never mind . . . what did you want to ask me?"

"I wondered if you—" Clint stopped, looked around, then said, "Could we step outside? It's noisy in here and I don't want to have to yell."

"Sure, why not?"

They went outside, Clarence leaving his beer on the bar.

"I was wondering if you had any ideas who might have been in that lynch party?" Clint asked.

"Why would I?"

"Maybe you heard somebody around town talking?" Clint asked. "Making threats? You must have talked to some people before you wrote your piece, to see how the town felt in general about what happened?"

"Well, I did, yeah," Clarence said. "I interviewed a bunch of people, and most of them were for the hanging. This was after the fact, mind you. I don't know how many of them would have been for it before it happened."

"Give me your best guess," Clint said. "Of all the people you spoke to, who was most for it?"

"Do you want to know the truth?"

"Of course."

"Women."

"What?"

"It was the women in town who were for it," the editor said. "Most of them said they wished it was their husbands who was in the lynch party. Said they'd be proud if it was."

"Jesus . . ."

"Yeah," Clarence said, "the death of a child—even a promiscuous child like Linda Kendall—sure brings the worst out in some women."

"Did the whole town know she was promiscuous?"

"Oh, sure . . . the women, anyway."

"And some of the men."

"Huh? Oh, yeah, you mean the ones she was with."

"I wonder how many there was?" Clint said. "I wonder how many of the women knew that their husbands had been with her?"

"What are you saying?" Clarence asked, with a look of disbelief. "That it was a woman who killed her?"

"Maybe more than one."

"And then what?"

"Then maybe it was women in the lynch party," Clint said. "Or maybe they goaded their husbands into it."

Clarence was frowning, but there was no longer disbelief on his face. He looked more like he'd just had a revelation.

"Women!" he said. "Could it be?"

"You tell me," Clint said. "You spoke to them after the fact. As a matter of fact, how did your wife feel about the whole thing?"

"My wife . . . she was for the lynching. She said any man who did that to a child—or even to a woman—deserved what he got."

"But how did she feel about Linda Kendall," Clint asked, "before all this happened."

Very suddenly Henry Clarence's demeanor changed. He looked . . . embarrassed about something.

"She thought Linda was a slut," he said. "She was always saying bad things about her."

"Why is that?"

Clarence didn't answer.

"Could it be she thought you'd slept with her?"

Clarence looked away.

"Oh, I see," Clint said. "You *had* been with her, and your wife knew."

"Yes."

"How did she find out?"

"Linda . . . told her." Suddenly, he got angry. "It was so stupid of her. The girl actually thought she was in love with me. Wanted me to leave my wife and take her away from here."

"And how did you feel about Linda?"

"Well . . . she was just a child, for Chrissake. I wasn't going to leave my wife, and the paper, for her."

"I see," Clint said, with sudden distaste for the man, "she was old enough to fuck, but not old enough for anything else."

"She was . . . young and . . . very . . . sexy in an earthy way," Clarence said, in an attempt to explain. "She'd come by the paper and . . . flirt . . ."

"And you'd flirt back?"

"Well, yes . . . it was . . . flattering to have a young girl like that come around," Clarence said. "One night she came by while I was locking up. We turned off the lights and . . . and started to just . . . play around and it got . . . got out of hand."

"And then it got out of hand how many more times after that?"

"She started to come by . . . a lot when I was closing."

"So you were involved with her," Clint said, "but you still don't think the lynched man—who I am now sure was my friend, Artie Bates—was guilty."

"One had nothing to do with the other," Clarence said. "He never had a trial, never had a chance to defend himself. If he had, and had been found guilty, I would have been in the front row at his hanging."

Clint stared at the man for a few moments.

"Well, what's wrong with you?"

"It strikes me that you have a very . . . warped sense of justice, Mr. Clarence," Clint said, "of what's right and what's wrong."

"Oh, come on," Clarence said, "you're a man, you've had young women—"

"Women," Clint said, cutting him off, "that's the operative word, Mr. Clarence. I've had young women . . . not young girls."

He left the editor standing there with his mouth open. He could no longer stand to be near the man.

THIRTY-TWO

"Tell me something," Clint said to Nell later. They had made love twice already, and were lying side-by-side, letting the sweat on their bodies dry.

"What?"

"How old was the youngest man you've ever been with?"

Without hesitating she said, "Twelve."

"What?"

"But I was eleven at the time," she said. "That's when I lost my virginity."

"Oh . . ."

"You mean, as an adult? What's the youngest man I ever slept with?"

"That's what I mean."

"What brought this on?"

He turned his head and looked at her, saw her looking at him with real interest.

"Linda Kendall."

"Oh."

"She was fourteen, right?"

"Yes."

"And she was sleeping with grown men."

137

"Apparently."

He hesitated, then said, "I talked with Henry Clarence."

"I know. Oh, you mean . . . he was with her?"

"Yes."

"Does his wife know?"

"Yes."

"Whoa," she said, looking at the ceiling. "No wonder they're fighting more lately." She looked at him again. "Wait a minute, are you feeling guilty about something?"

"Maybe."

"Were you ever with a girl that much younger than you?"

"Well . . . no, not *that* much younger."

"But younger?"

"Yes."

"And now you're feeling guilty about it?"

"I'm just . . . thinking back."

"You're nothing like Henry Clarence, Clint," Nell said. "In fact, you're nothing like any man I've ever known. You've got nothing to feel guilty about."

"Maybe not . . ."

"What else is on your mind?"

"Something I said to Henry tonight."

"Which is?"

"That it might have been a woman who killed Linda Kendall," he said, "and it might have been a bunch of women who lynched Artie Bates."

"Women?"

"Who else would get angry enough at what happened to that girl?" Clint asked. "Women, with children of their own."

"Or even a woman without children," she said.

Now he turned his head and looked at her.

"Nell . . ."

"I know she was a slut," Nell said, sadly, "but she was still a fourteen-year-old child."

"And could you have killed the man who killed her?"

"Oh, yes," she said. "If he'd been arrested, tried and convicted or—even better—confessed, I would have liked to be the one to throw the switch, open that trap door and drop him."

"But you would have needed proof first."

"Of course."

"Well, somebody in this town didn't need proof," Clint said.

"And you think it was women?"

"What if a woman killed her, and then incited her husband to form the lynch mob. It only ever takes one man with a rope and a big mouth. I've seen it happen countless times."

"I guess that could be."

"You know the women in this town, Nell," he said. "Who'd be your best guess?"

"Oh, hey," Nell said, "you gotta know the women in this town don't exactly take to me."

"Why not?" he asked. "You don't run a whorehouse, you run a legitimate business."

"Oh, yeah, well tell them that," she said. "All they know is that their husbands come to my place and leave with a lot less money."

"You must know somebody," he said, "just a woman who was upset enough to do something about it?"

"Well . . . there's only one woman I can think of."

"Who's that?"

She looked at him and said, "Jenny Kendall."

Clint slipped out of bed later, while Nell was asleep, and went out to the bar in the saloon to get himself a beer. He lit a lamp, took it to the bar, then took it and the beer over to Nell's table.

He wanted to examine this theory a little further. Could

it be possible for a bunch of women to have done something like this? He'd seen men do it many times, but women? Or was he just reaching? Maybe he should stick with the theory that said one woman incited one man to incite a lynch mob.

Jenny Kendall? The girl's mother?

Why had that never occurred to him before?

THIRTY-THREE

Marshal John Dean looked up as Clint entered his office.

"I heard you were back."

"Did you?"

"You don't seem to be spending too much time in your hotel room," Dean said. "I went over there this morning."

"Well, I'm here now," Clint said. "What did you want to see me about?"

"I was just wondering what you found out in Benson's Fork."

"What makes you think I went there?"

"Where else would you have gone when you left here?" he asked. "You were headed in that direction, weren't you?"

Clint stared at him, then said, "You were watching me, weren't you? When those three yahoos braced me, you were watching."

"You did a pretty fair job of backing them down."

"Did you know them?"

"Never saw them before."

"Did you talk to them after I left?"

"What for?"

"Are they still in town?"

"Haven't seen them."

"Mind if I sit?"

"I'd prefer it. My neck's getting tired."

Clint sat across from the man.

"You lied to me."

"About what?"

"About there being a deputy marshal in Benson's Fork."

Dean thought a moment, then said, "I don't think I lied to you. I think I said there was an office there for a deputy, but I don't recall ever saying that there was a deputy there now."

Clint knew they could have this argument all day, and it really didn't matter much.

"I learned that most of the merchants in Benson's Fork knew Artie Bates, and liked him. He bought all of his supplies there, apparently."

"I see."

"He said this town was too big and noisy for him."

"Which means he had been here at one time or another."

"Right."

"Well," Dean said, "maybe somebody in town knows him, but I don't know who it would be."

"Tell me something, Marshal."

"If I can."

"Do you have any ideas about who might have been in that lynch party?"

"Are you convinced it was your friend they lynched?"

"Pretty much," Clint said. "About the only way to really cinch it would be to dig him up. I don't know that I want to do that. Will you answer my question?"

Dean pursed his lips and thought a moment.

"The answer is yes, I do have some thoughts about it," he said, "but the answer to your next question is no, I won't give you any names."

"Why not?"

"Because I have no proof they were involved."

"There was no proof against Artie Bates, either," Clint said, "and yet he was hanged."

"Not by me."

"You could have stopped it."

"I told you I wasn't there."

"Did you know about it?"

"No!" Dean said, a little too fast. "If I had known I would have stopped it."

Clint couldn't tell if the man was being truthful or not. The question perturbed him, though, on some level. Guilt, maybe one way or the other.

"Okay, let me ask you this," Clint said. "Could the lynch party have been made up of women?"

Dean stared at him a moment, then said, "What?"

"Women," Clint said. "Maybe the women in town got tired of the men not doing anything and took matters into their own hands?"

"That's . . . ridiculous! Absurd! Where did you ever get an idea like that?" the lawman demanded.

"It just sort of popped into my head," Clint said. "And I thought of something else, too."

"I can't wait to hear it."

"What if a woman killed Linda Kendall?" he asked. "After all, she'd slept around town. Maybe somebody's wife found out and got mad enough to do her in."

Dean scratched his head then ran his hand over his mouth.

"That's not as far-fetched as your other idea," he said, finally. "I thought of that myself."

"Did you look into it?"

"No," he said, "not after the lynching."

"Why not?"

Dean didn't answer.

"Did Allan Kendall order you to let it drop?"

"He didn't order me!" Dean snapped. "He . . . suggested that I let it lie. After all, he was the girl's father."

"Stepfather," Clint corrected him. "Did you ever ask the mother if she wanted it dropped?"

"No," Dean said, "I never spoke with the mother."

"Why not?"

"Mr. Kendall . . . said she wasn't up to it."

"Marshal," Clint said, "I'd like to talk to Jenny Kendall."

"That's not possible. Why would you want to do that? Bring it all back for her? That would be cruel."

"Do you really think she's forgotten about it, already?" Clint asked. "And don't you think it's even more cruel to let her go on thinking the man who killed her daughter has paid for it if he hasn't?"

Again, Dean didn't answer.

Clint stood up.

"I'm going to give you some time to think this over, Marshal," he said. "I think you know that Artie Bates wasn't guilty. I think it's eating away at you that he was lynched and you didn't do anything about—whether you knew about it or not ahead of time, you haven't done anything about it since."

Clint turned and walked to the door. He opened it, then with his hand on the doorknob looked at the Marshal.

"What do you know about me?" Dean asked. "You don't know anything about me, Adams."

"I get the feeling you're not all the way in Kendall's pocket, Marshal," Clint said. "There's still time for you to do the right thing."

The two men stared at each other for a while, and then Clint went out the door, closing it gently behind him.

THIRTY-FOUR

Clint decided to give Dean the better part of the day to come to terms with himself and what he should do. He wasn't going to try to go out and see Jenny Kendall alone unless he absolutely had to. He may have made three ranch hands back down, but there would be a lot more than three out there.

"Are you Clint Adams?"

He turned and looked at the woman who had spoken. She was blonde, in her early thirties. She had a good body and a face that had been very pretty at one time, but something—anger? bitterness?—had etched lines where they shouldn't have been on a woman her age.

"I'm Clint Adams."

"I'd like to talk to you."

"Ma'am," he said, "I'm a little busy—"

"I was going to talk to the marshal," she went on, "but it was about you, and since you're here now—unless you'd rather I talk to the marshal?"

"Well, I don't know, Ma'am," he said. "What's it about and . . . and who are you?"

"My name is Kate," she said, "Kate Clarence."

"Clarence . . . you mean—"

"That's right," she said. "Henry Clarence is my husband. I own the *Sioux City Gazette,* Mr. Adams."

"Why not, Mrs. Clarence," he said. "Over a cup of coffee, or tea?"

"Coffee would be fine."

"Do you know a place . . ."

"Follow me," she said. "There's a small café not far from here."

"Lead the way."

When they had coffee and pie in front of them she leaned forward and said intently, "I want you to leave my husband alone."

"Exactly what is it you think I'm doing to your husband, Mrs. Clarence?"

"He came home upset last night," she said. "Agitated. I'd never seen him like that. When I asked him what was wrong, he told me about the conversation you and he had had."

Clint couldn't believe that Clarence would have told her *everything* they talked about.

"I'm not sure I understand—"

"Oh, come now, Mr. Adams," she said. "We're adults here. I know about my husband and that . . . that girl."

"Linda Kendall?"

"Yes." The lines of bitterness at the corners of her mouth deepened. They were ugly. Her bitterness was ugly. Why do women want to hang onto things—men, marriages— that make them bitter and ugly?

"How much do you—"

"I know everything there is to know!" she blurted. "All right?" She looked around, then lowered her voice even though there was no one else in the café at that time of the day. "I know it all."

"What do you want from me, Mrs. Clarence?"

"I don't want you to tell anyone our . . . our problems."

"Your secrets?"

"All right, yes, our secrets," she said. "If you do—if you tell, I'll use my newspaper to make you sorry."

He laughed, because the woman was so intent on saving what was left of her laughable relationship with her husband.

"What will you do to me, Mrs. Clarence?" he asked. "Ruin my reputation? Have you looked at my reputation lately? Anything you do to it would probably be an improvement."

"So then . . . you're going to tell?"

"Who would I tell, and why?" he asked. "What good would it do me? It seems to me the two of you know, and that's bad enough. What happens with your marriage is your business. I want no part of it."

He stood up then, because he'd had enough of this bitter, desperate woman and her threats.

"I will say this, though," he added. "I don't know why you'd want to stay with him after what he did with that girl."

She covered her face with one fist, but said, "He didn't do anything dozens of other men in this town hadn't done."

"Okay, then," Clint said, "that makes it okay," and left.

THIRTY-FIVE

Clarence must have gone back home to his wife after their talk last night, instead of going with one of Nell's girls. Why would the man have told his wife what they talked about? Guilt? Or had he asked her the same hard questions Clint had asked him? Could a woman have killed Linda Kendall? Could a group of women have lynched Artie Bates? Or could a woman have egged her man on to form the lynch party? And if any of this was true, what women?

Clint had walked away from Henry Clarence in disgust last night, but in the light of day he knew he had no right to judge the man. He'd been with some pretty young girls in the past few years, girls who wanted to be with him, but still young girls—eighteen, nineteen . . . not fourteen, but what if a beautiful fourteen-year-old had come to him and presented herself to him. In a weak moment, what would he have done?

Of course, Henry Clarence wasn't guilty of one weak moment, but many.

Clint walked to the newspaper office and found it unlocked. He walked in. Henry Clarence was bending over the press, cursing it. He saw Clint and stood straight up.

"You know," he said, "if I were working at a real paper in a real city, I wouldn't have to do this. They have people who do this, you know."

"I know."

"What can I do for you today? Want to judge me some more?"

"I came to apologize," Clint said. "I had no right to judge you last night, or any day."

"Forget it," Clarence said. "I've judged myself plenty, even before poor Linda's death."

"Were you still . . . seeing her when she died?"

"No," he said, "I'd stopped. It wasn't easy, but I made myself stop. See, I really do love my wife. But she's gotten so . . . bitter over the past few years and she's sort of . . . dried up, if you know what I mean."

"I think I do," Clint said. "I met your wife."

"What? You met Kate?"

"That's right."

"When?"

"This morning," Clint said. "She was on her way to the marshal's office."

"What was she goin' there for?"

"To talk to him about keeping me away from you."

"Jesus," he said, wiping his hands on a rag, and then running his hands over his face. "I was drunk last night, went home, talked to much . . . what happened? This morning, I mean."

"I happened to be coming out of the marshal's office. She and I went for a cup of coffee. She's a very sad woman."

"Maybe she's got a right to be sad," he said, "and bitter, I don't know."

"Henry," Clint said, "do you think your wife could have killed Linda?"

Clarence had been looking down at his feet and at that question his head shot up, his eyes wide.

"No!" he said, but it was plain in his face—the fear— that he'd often thought about it himself.

"You were afraid she had, weren't you?" Clint asked.

Clarence hesitated, then said, "For a while, yes."

"And what changed your mind?"

"I . . . stopped thinking about it."

"Which means you didn't change your mind?"

"Which means I stopped thinking about it."

"But you want to know the truth, Henry, or you wouldn't have egged me on when we first met."

"That's true. I—" He stopped short and looked over Clint's shoulder. Clint turned and saw Marshal John Dean standing in the doorway.

"Marshal," he said.

"John," Clarence said, "something I can do for you?"

"No, Henry," Dean said, "I was looking for Mr. Adams." He looked at Clint. "Got a minute?"

"Sure." He looked at Clarence, who seemed nervous now. Was Clint going to tell Dean what they had just been talking about? "Excuse me."

"Sure."

Clint turned and walked to the door. Dean stepped outside to wait for him.

"What is it Marshal?"

"You still want to have that talk with Jenny Kendall?"

"Yes, I do."

"Come on, then," he said. "I'll go out there with you."

"What changed your mind?"

Dean glared at him and said, "Don't look a gift horse in the mouth, Adams. Just come on."

THIRTY-SIX

When they rode up to the Kendall ranch they were met by the foreman, Walker. He was backed by a half a dozen hands with guns. Clint didn't think they knew they were coming, he just thought Kendall was keeping his men on the alert.

"What can we do for you, Marshal?" Walker asked.

"We're here to see Mr. Kendall, Walker."

"You and him?"

"That's right."

"What's it about?"

"We'll tell Mr. Kendall that."

Walker studied the two men for a few moments, then turned to his men and said, "Keep an eye on them."

"You don't need all these men, Walker," Marshal Dean said.

Walker looked at Dean, then at his men and repeated, "Watch 'em."

He went into the house, straight to his boss's office.

Upstairs on the second floor Jenny Kendall looked out, saw the two men on horseback. She could see the light reflecting off the badge one of them wore. That would be Marshal John Dean. He was the man who was supposed to find out who killed her little girl.

She turned from her window and started from the room.

"Adams and the marshal?" Kendall asked.

"That's right," Walker said, "and the marshal is tryin' to act like a real lawman, Boss."

"Is that a fact?" Kendall asked. "I guess he's forgotten whose pocket he's in, eh, Walker?"

"Looks like it."

"All right," Kendall said, getting up from behind his desk, "I'll go and see them outside. Keep your men and their guns handy."

"Yes, sir."

"And when are those other men coming in?"

"I got an answer to my telegram today," Walker said. "They'll be here tomorrow."

"Understand this," Allan Kendall said. "No matter what happens today, I want those men to do their job tomorrow. All right?"

"Yes, sir," Walker said. "Tomorrow, no matter what happens."

"Let's go."

Kendall and Walker walked into the entry foyer just as Jenny Kendall started down the stairs. She saw them too late to run, or hide.

When Kendall saw his wife he grew angry.

"What are you doing out of your room?" he demanded.

"Those men outside—"

"The men outside are none of your business," Kendall said. "They're mine. Get back upstairs."

"But one of them is the marshal—"

"Back upstairs, Jenny!" he shouted. "Don't come back down unless I call for you. Understand?"

Jenny became bold, just for a moment.

"I am not one of your men, Allan Kendall," she said. "You can't order me around."

Kendall stared at her, a look designed to melt all of her resolve away, and it worked—as it always did.

"Jenny," he said, slowly, "go back up to your room before I have Walker take you back."

She glared at him, but her boldness was gone. She turned, shoulders slumped, and walked back up the stairs.

"All right," Kendall said to Walker, "let's go outside and see why the marshal is acting like a real lawman."

THIRTY-SEVEN

Kendall came down the steps with Walker and they both stood in front of the men with the guns. Some of the hands had rifles, others were simply wearing guns and holsters.

"I understand you want to see me," Kendall said, looking at Clint first, and then at Dean. "Marshal, I'm a little surprised at the company you're keeping these days."

"I thought it better to come out here with Adams then to let him come out alone, Mr. Kendall."

"Well," Kendall said, "why are the two of you out here at all?"

"We want to talk to Mrs. Kendall."

That surprised Kendall. Clint could see it on the man's face.

"What the hell for?" he asked. "What's this about?"

"It's about Artemus Bates, Mr. Kendall," Clint said.

"Who the hell is Artemus Bates?"

"He's a friend of mine," Clint said, "and the man who was lynched for your stepdaughter's murder."

"And he deserved it," Walker said, and the hands behind him agreed.

"He deserved a trial," Clint said, "and a chance to prove his innocence."

157

"He wasn't innocent!" one of the ranch hands chimed in.

"He had a right to have a chance to prove that," Clint said. "A lynch party took that right away from him."

"Dean, what the hell is going on? You know my wife doesn't want to talk about this."

"No, I don't know that, Mr. Kendall," Dean said. "You see, I never talked to your wife after the murder, or after the lynching, and I should have. You see, I haven't exactly been doing my job, up to now, but that's going to change."

Kendall stared at Dean, then at Clint, then back at Dean again.

"Marshal," Kendall said, then, "I think maybe you and I need to have a talk . . . alone."

"I don't think so, Mr. Kendall," Dean said. "I think what we need to do is talk with your wife."

"I think we need to talk about your political career," Kendall said, tightly.

"My political career is later, Mr. Kendall," Dean said. Clint had the feeling that this was going to cost the man a lot. He only hoped it would be worth it, in the end. "This is now."

"You're making a big mistake, Marshal."

"This badge gives me the right to make a whole lot of mistakes, Mr. Kendall," Dean said.

"This is a very bad one."

"It may very well turn out to be," the Marshal said, "but we'd like to talk to your wife . . . now."

Kendall glared at them and Clint wondered if he was going to sic his men on them. He wondered how many of these ranch hands were willing to take part in gunplay against the law. He wondered if any of them had been willing to be part of a lynch party, to hang an innocent man.

"All right," Kendall said, finally, but he was shaking with rage. "I'll have to talk to her first, prepare her."

"That's fine," Dean said, "but before you go I want you

to disperse these men. Tell them to put up their guns and go back to work."

"I have a right to protect myself—"

"Not against me."

Kendall glared at Dean with hatred. He had never imagined that the man had this much backbone. Part of it had to be that he was backed by the Gunsmith, or else Dean would never have pulled this.

He was going to pay dearly for this affront.

"All right," Kendall said, finally. "Walker, have the men go back to work."

"But Boss—"

"Do as I tell you!"

"Yes, sir."

As the men were dispersing, and Allan Kendall was mounting the steps to enter the house, Clint heard the marshal heave a huge sigh of relief.

"Well done, Marshal," he said, so only the lawman could hear him. "Bravo."

THIRTY-EIGHT

"Good," Jenny Kendall said, "good, someone stood up to you. They want to talk to me."

"Jenny, sweetheart," Allan Kendall said, "you have to be careful what you say to these people. This could be very dangerous for us."

"As dangerous as it was for my Linda?"

"Linda was a slut, Jenny," Kendall said. "We knew that for a long time."

"She was like that," Jenny said, "only because I failed her." She was sitting on their bed with her hands folded in her lap. "It was my fault, not hers. She didn't deserve to . . . die like that."

"Jenny," Kendall said, "take care. You don't want to make me angry, do you?"

She didn't answer.

He put his hand beneath her chin and tilted her head up, so that she had to look at him.

"Do you?"

She hesitated, then said, "N-no."

"That's good. So you'll be very careful about what you say to these people?" he asked.

"Y-yes."

"There," he said, sliding his hand away from her chin and down her arm. "That's better."

She shivered as he took his hand away from her.

"We'll go down to the living room and you can talk to them there," he said, taking her hands and drawing her to her feet. "I'll be with you every moment."

She stood up, her shoulders still hunched, unsure as to whether or not he was going to strike her. He knew how to hit her and not have any marks show. He'd proved it many times before.

"Come," he said, leading her to the door, "that's my girl. It'll be all right. Once we get rid of them it will be all right, hmm?"

"Y-yes, Allan."

"There's my good girl."

He took hold of one of her arms, holding it tightly. She'd lost a lot of weight recently, and her arm felt like a twig. He could snap it like a twig, too, if he wanted to. After all, she belonged to him.

"You know Marshal Dean," he said, as they moved down the hall, "the other man's name is Clint Adams. You don't have to speak to him at all, do you understand? Just to the marshal."

"I understand."

"I know that you do." He squeezed her arm tighter, forgetting himself, and when she whimpered he released it—but the damage was done.

There were red fingermarks on her arm.

THIRTY-NINE

"What do you think he's telling her right now?" Clint asked.

"I guess that depends on what he's guilty of," Dean said.

The men had dispersed and the only one left was Walker, waiting with his arms folded.

"That's what we want to find out," Clint said. "He's hiding something, I know that much."

"How?"

"Men with money," Clint said, "always have something to hide."

"I hope this pans out, Adams," Dean said. "I get the feeling I just dumped my political career."

"You don't need Kendall for that, Marshal."

"I don't?"

"Nope," Clint said. "You just showed me everything you'll need to get ahead in politics."

Dean sighed and said, "I hope you're right."

Kendall left his wife in the living room and went out to get Clint and Marshal Dean.

"She's very fragile," he said to them. "If she begins to get distressed I'll have to ask you to stop."

"We understand," Dean said.

"Very well," Kendall said. "Follow me."

The three of them started up the steps, and Walker began to follow. Kendall stopped and looked at his foreman.

"Not you, Walker," Kendall said. "See to the men."

"But, Mr. Kendall—"

"You heard me," Kendall said. "Do your job."

"Yes, sir."

"Gentlemen," Kendall said, as polite as he could be, "this way."

"My dear," Kendall said, as the three men entered the living room, "I believe you remember the marshal."

"Yes," Jenny Kendall said, rising from the chair she'd been sitting in. "Hello, Marshal Dean."

When Kendall did not introduce Clint, the marshal did.

"This is Clint Adams, Mrs. Kendall."

"A pleasure to meet you, Mr. Adams."

"The pleasure is mine, Ma'am," Clint said. He saw the red fingermarks on her arm and felt the anger starting in the pit of his stomach. He hated men who mistreated women.

"Please," the marshal said to her, "sit down."

"I'm a poor hostess," she said. "Can I offer you gentlemen some tea, or something?"

"No, Ma'am," Dean said. "We won't keep you long. We just have some questions for you."

"All right," she said, and sat down. All three men remained standing. Clint felt badly, but he thought that this might intimidate her enough to give them the answers they were after.

"Ma'am," John Dean said, "I hate to bring this subject up, and if it distresses you please let me know—"

"Marshal," she said, "if we are going to talk about the

death of my daughter I assure you it *will* distress me, but I will go on with it."

"You're very brave, Ma'am."

Her eyes darted to her husband and she said, "Not at all."

Dean looked at Clint. They had agreed beforehand that the lawman should be the one to ask the questions. During the ride out Clint had told the man the things he wanted to know.

". . . if we can get the right answers," Clint had said, after explaining, "I think we'll be able to find out the truth."

"I have to say it makes sense," Dean said. "It also makes me ashamed I never asked these things before."

"Marshal," Clint said, "sometimes it just takes an outsider to come in and shake things up."

"Outsiders usually shake things up in a town," Dean had said, "but I'm starting to realize that's their job."

"Well," Clint had replied, "let's hope I do mine well."

"And I do mine," Dean added. "I don't think I've done it particularly well in some time."

"That's why we all get second chances, Marshal," Clint said. "All we have to do is make the most of them."

"I'll give it my best shot," Dean had said.

Clint looked at Jenny Kendall as Marshal Dean prepared to ask his questions. He *knew* that she had been prepared in some way by her husband. He only hoped that she would be able to find some way to tell the truth.

FORTY

"Mrs. Kendall," Dean said, "do you think the man who was hung was the man who killed your daughter?"

"Now wait a minute—" Kendall started.

"It's a fair question, Mr. Kendall," Clint said. "We just want to know if your wife is satisfied that the guilty party paid for his crime."

"You have no authority, here," Kendall said, pointing his index finger at Clint.

"He's here with me," Dean said.

Kendall pointed the same finger at Dean, as if it were the most powerful weapon in his arsenal.

"You're going to be sorry for this!"

"Stop it, Allan," Jenny Kendall said.

"What?"

"Stop bellowing," she said. "You do that all the time. It's how you get your way in business, and it's how you get your way with me. I won't have anymore, do you hear? I won't."

"Well," Kendall said, "the little mouse grows fangs?"

She stood up, turned and faced her husband.

"These men are concerned about what happened to Linda," she said. "Are you?"

"Jenny," Kendall said, his tone softer, "you know I'm sorry for what happened to Linda—"

"And that poor man?" Jenny asked. "Are you sorry for that poor man who was lynched?"

She turned to look at Dean and Clint.

"Did he have any family, that man?"

"If it's who we think it was," Clint said, "no. But he was my friend."

"Then I'm sorry for your loss," Jenny said.

"Jenny," Kendall said, "you'll get agitated."

"You agitate me, Allan," she said, "not these men."

Suddenly a sneer appeared on the face of Allan Kendall.

"You're very brave when they're here, aren't you, Jenny?" he demanded. "You're not that brave when it's just you and me, are you?"

"No, I'm not," she said to him, then turned to Clint and Dean and asked, "Do you know why?"

Clint thought he did, but he said, "Why?"

"Because when no one else is around he can hit me," she said, "and I don't like getting hit. I don't like it at all. It frightens me." She turned and looked at her husband. "But what happened to Linda frightens me even more— and what happened to that poor man."

"Mrs. Kendall," Dean asked, "are you saying that the man who was lynched did not kill your daughter?"

"Yes, Marshal Dean," she replied, "that's exactly what I'm saying."

"And do you know who did kill her?"

"God help me," she said, and then sobbed, "I do."

"Now see what you've done," Kendall said. "You've upset her."

"I don't think it's us who are upsetting her, Mr. Kendall," Dean said. "I'll have to ask you to be quiet now."

"But, you can't—"

"You'll have to be quiet or I'll put you out."

"You can't put me out of my own home!"

"Try me!"

Kendall was faced with something he'd never been faced with before—backbone. It was coming from the marshal, and from his own wife, and he didn't know how to handle it.

Jenny Kendall had gained control of herself.

"Mrs. Kendall," Marshal Dean asked, "can you tell us who killed your daughter, Linda?"

"Yes, Marshal, I can," she said, "and may God forgive me for not coming forward and saying it before this." She pointed a shaky finger at Allan Kendall. "He did—he killed his own stepdaughter."

"And you, you stupid bitch," Allan Kendall said, "you've just killed yourself, and everyone in this room!"

FORTY-ONE

"You're under arrest, Mr. Kendall," Marshal Dean said.

"This is crazy," Kendall said. "You can't believe a word she says. She's . . . distraught. She hasn't been in her right mind since . . . since her daughter was killed."

"Since you killed her, you mean," Jenny said, "and since you let that man be lynched for it."

"Why did you do it, Kendall?" Dean asked.

Kendall kept silent.

"They were . . . sleeping together," Jenny said. "They thought I didn't know, but I did."

"The stupid little bitch thought I was going to marry her," Kendall said. "She was fourteen years old!"

"That's the whole point, Kendall," Clint said.

"Ah," Kendall said, "can either of you tell me you wouldn't have done the same? Look at the mother, dried out and useless. Linda was alive and full of vitality. Either one of you would have done the same."

"Not with a fourteen-year-old," Clint said. "Sorry, but not me."

"Dean, you saw her. You know what she looked like . . . what she was like."

"Sorry, Kendall," the marshal said, "she looked fourteen to me."

"Mrs. Kendall," Clint asked, "do you know who was in that lynch party?"

"No, Mr. Adams, I don't," she said. "I wish I did—but I can tell you one thing. It was his idea."

"Goddamnit, woman!" Kendall shouted.

"That's enough, Kendall," Dean said. "You're coming with us to town."

"You'll never get me off this property," Kendall said. "My men won't hear of it."

Dean looked at Clint.

"He might be right."

"Look," Clint said, "there were what—five or six men in that lynch party? That's probably all we have to deal with."

"Great," Dean said, "three-to-one odds."

"Maybe not," Clint said. "Let's get Walker in here."

"You think he'll help?"

"No," Clint said. "I think he's one of the lynch party. Getting him in here will cut down on the odds."

"Good idea." Kendall opened his mouth, maybe to say something, maybe to yell a warning, but Dean saw it. "If you open your mouth I'll shoot you in the knee."

"You're shooting yourself in the foot, here, Marshal," Kendall said. "I could have helped you, politically."

"I know that, Kendall," Dean said. "Why do you think I'm so angry with you?" He looked at Clint. "Go ahead, get Walker."

"Right."

Clint was almost to the front door when he realized what a chance he was taking. By leaving Dean alone with Kendall he was giving the two men a chance to talk. Could Kendall convince the marshal to help him? Would he offer him money as well as help in the political arena? When Clint came back in would it be to a trap?

He opened the front door and stepped out. Walker was standing at the bottom of the steps.

"Walker?"

"Yeah?"

"Your boss wants you inside."

Walker came up the steps and moved past Clint into the house.

"It's about time—wha—"

Clint quickly relieved the man of his gun, plucking it from his holster and training it on him.

"What the hell—"

"Just move," he said. "Into the living room."

Clint led Walker into the room at gunpoint. The position of the three people had not changed. Surely, if Kendall and Dean had hatched a plot against him Jenny Kendall would warn him, wouldn't he? Unless they had threatened to kill her? But now that she had spoken up against her husband, would such a threat keep her silent?

As he entered the three people looked at him and Walker. Clint looked at Dean and made a snap judgment about the man, one that may well have ended up costing him his life if he was wrong.

"What's going on, Mr. Kendall?" Walker asked.

"Your boss is under arrest, Walker," Dean said.

"For what?"

"The rape and murder of Linda Kendall."

"There was no rape!" Kendall said, as if that charge were more serious than the other.

"He's right about that," Jenny said. "God forgive me for saying this, but no man ever had to rape my daughter. She gave herself away freely."

Clint and Dean both looked at Walker.

"Hey, not to me," Walker said. "I never touched her."

"Did you know her boss had killed her?" Dean asked.

"Don't answer that, Walker!"

Walker looked around the room, confused.

"Can we make a deal?" he asked the marshal.

"What kind of deal?"

"I don't want to go to jail."

"You won't go to jail for the girl," Dean said. "Just tell us what happened."

"I don't know anything until after she was dead," Walker said, "and then I just helped dump the body."

"Walker! You're a dead man!"

"He can't hurt you from a cell, Walker," Dean said.

"What happened out at the house, Walker?" Clint asked. "The day of the lynching?"

"I went out there with five of the men," Walker said. "We had our faces covered, and we had a rope, but we never intended to hang him."

"It just got out of hand, huh?" Clint asked.

"That's right," Walker said, "it did. I don't know what happened, but suddenly they were stringing him up to a tree and I couldn't do anything to stop it."

"But you tried, huh?" Clint asked.

Walker looked away.

"Maybe not hard enough—but by that time it was too late. I thought if I really tried to stop them they'd . . . they'd turn on me."

"You just put yourself in prison, you idiot!" Kendall said.

"He said I wouldn't go to jail!" Walker said, pointing to the marshal.

"Not for the girl," Dean said. "I'll tell the judge you cooperated."

"See?" Walker said to Kendall.

"But for the lynching," Clint said. "For that, you'll go to jail."

"And *you'll* be the one who hangs!" Kendall said.

"Wait a minute, wait a minute!" Walker said. "We can still make a deal."

"What do you have to deal with?" Dean asked.

"The others," Walker said, desperately. "I can give you the names of the others in the lynch party."

Dean and Clint exchanged a glance and then Dean said to Walker, "Okay, maybe we can do some business . . ."

FORTY-TWO

"This ain't fair!" Walker shouted from his cell.

"Idiot!" Kendall said from his.

"Shut up in there!" Dean shouted.

Clint was surprised at Dean's anger, but he supposed that the man had a lot to be angry about. After all, he felt this incident was going to hurt his chance to go into politics. Clint, on the other hand, felt that when the word got out it would help him, and he tried to convince Dean of this.

"Look at what happened." Clint said. "You walked right into Allan Kendall's home and took him out in front of all his men. You arrested him, with no regard for what it would mean to your future."

"Don't remind me."

"Come on," Clint said. "you did the right thing. You're a hero—or you will be when the newspapers get hold of you."

"You think so?"

"In fact," Clint said, "I'll bet our local newspaper editor, Henry Clarence, would love to do a story on the whole thing."

"Well," Dean said, "once I tell him you were there—"

"Don't tell him that."

"What?"

"Don't tell anyone."

"You mean . . . take all the credit?'

"Why not? You're the lawman. I was just along as another gun. Anybody could have done it."

"I don't think anybody could have walked Kendall and Walker out of there the way we did, with all his men there. I mean, they knew who you were."

"They knew their boss would pay for it if they pulled anything," Clint said. "They want to keep their jobs, most of them."

"What about the names we got from Walker?" Dean asked. "The other members of the lynch party?"

"Appoint yourself some deputies and pick them up later, one at a time, so there won't be a chance of gunplay."

"And you don't mind if I take all the credit?"

"Not only don't I mind," Clint said, "I insist on it."

"Well . . . okay, if you insist."

Clint stood up to leave and Dean said, "Answer a question for me?'

"Sure."

"When you went outside to get Walker?"

"Yeah?"

"Did you think I'd turn on you when you came back in?"

"I thought about it," Clint said, "but I decided you wouldn't."

"Why? Why'd you decide that?"

"I made a quick judgment right there and then," Clint said. "I thought you were sincere when you came to me this morning."

"It could have been a trap all the way."

"It could have been," Clint said. "In fact, the whole time

ne's in your jail Kendall's going to be upping his offer, you
know."

"I know."

"At some point it may be hard to resist."

"I think I'll manage," Dean said. "I draw the line at
working for a man who'd kill his own daughter—even if
t was his stepdaughter. How about that Mrs. Kendall? A
brave woman, huh?"

"She doesn't think so," Clint said. "She thinks her cow-
ardice ultimately cost her daughter her life."

"Well," Dean said, "maybe it did. I mean, if she knew
all along . . ."

"She was afraid of her husband, Marshal," Clint said.
"With us around she was able to find the courage to speak,
but . . ."

Both men stood there awkwardly, knowing that the
whole mess could have been averted. The girl would be
alive if the mother had put her foot down, and Artie Bates
would be alive, as well.

Suddenly, Dean put his hand out and Clint took it.

"Thanks."

"For what?"

"Turning me around, I guess," the man said. "I kept
thinking I wasn't in Kendall's pocket, but I guess I was
slipping further and further in all the time."

"You would have found your way out."

"Maybe," Dean said, "maybe not."

Clint walked to the door.

"When will you be leaving?"

"Sometime tomorrow, I guess," Clint said. "I've done
what I wanted to do. I'd like to put this town behind me."

"I don't blame you." Dean said. "Stop by in the morning."

"Sure."

Clint left, started to his hotel, then detoured and headed for Nell's.

"Could have saved a lot of money on the hotel," Nell said. Cuddling up to him in her bed, later."

"Who knew?" He put his arm around her, stroked the warm skin of her shoulder and arm.

"Do you have to leave tomorrow?" she asked.

"Except for you," he said, "there are no pleasant memories here. Plus, I've got to return a horse to French Creek. Turns out it was in a corral out at the Kendall ranch."

They laid there in silence for a few moments, and then she was, "That poor woman."

"That poor woman could have saved her daughter's life," Clint said. "I don't have any sympathy for her."

"You're a hard man," Nell said. "She lost her daughter, and now her husband."

"So now she's a rich woman without an abusive husband and amoral daughter around," Clint said. "Tough life ahead."

FORTY-THREE

Clint did stop by the Marshal's office the next morning, but briefly. The two men shook hands again and Dean assured him that his "two guests" were still in their rooms and would be until the judge came to town.

"I never doubted it," Clint said.

He left the office and saw Henry Clarence, the editor of the paper, almost running towards him. He prepared himself to stave off the man's requests for an interview before he left town.

"Are you leaving town?"

"Within minutes," Clint said, thinking this might put the man off.

"Is he in?" Clarence asked.

"The marshal? Yeah, he's there."

"This is some story," the man said, breathless. "Did you hear that he arrested Allan Kendall last night?"

"I did hear that, yeah."

"This proves that your friend was innocent."

"Yes, it does."

"Well, I'm gonna do a big story on Marshal Dean arresting Kendall and his foreman, Walker, but I'll also do a side piece clearing your friend."

"That's real nice of you, Mr. Clarence. I appreciate it."

"Hey," Clarence said, "I'm just trying to report the truth. That's what I've wanted to do all along."

"Well, I admire you for it," Clint said, "and I wish you good luck."

"Thanks."

The two men looked at each other for a few moments, and Clint thought the man realized that he was wishing him good luck for more than just running his newspaper.

"Good luck to you, too," the man said, and rushed into the marshal's office.

Clint turned and walked toward the livery.

Having recovered the gray mare he'd rented in French Creek he was going to bring that animal back there before he left Minnesota. He still needed another horse, though, and knew he wasn't going to find one in French Creek, so he tried to make a deal with the liveryman for the gelding he'd been riding the past couple of days.

"Take it," the man said.

"I'll pay you for it."

"I'd rather you jest take 'im, Mr. Adams," the man said. "Sorta my way of makin' amends."

Clint didn't think the man needed to make amends, but he decided not to argue the point. He saddled the gelding, attached a lead rope to the mare, and rode out of the livery, and out of Sioux City.

FORTY-FOUR

On the way back to French Creek Clint detoured to stop at Artie Bates's house again. Now that he knew for sure his friend was the man who had been lynched he felt a responsibility to go through the house, just in case there was anything of value there. As it turned out, after going through the ransacked house, he found nothing. It seemed Bates didn't own anything of value, which made Clint even sadder.

He went to the front doorway and angrily tore the door off the remaining hinge. As he threw the door outside he heard a shot and a bullet struck the wall near his head. He reacted immediately as a hail of bullets followed the first. As he lay prone on the floor the bullets chewed up the inside of the house, destroying whatever had not been destroyed the first time. Clint wondered if the men who were firing at him were members of the lynch party that day, or some new guns hired by Allan Kendall—because he had no doubt that these men worked for Kendall. They had probably been hired—through Walker—before he had been arrested. Maybe they didn't know their employer was in jail.

He waited for the firing to stop and then lifted his head. He did not draw his gun yet because there was nothing for him to fire at.

"Hello outside!"

There was silence, followed by an answering voice.

"Whataya want?"

"I think you boys should know your boss is in jail in Sioux City. The party's over and there's nobody to pay you."

They opened fire again and he put his head down and waited it out.

"Guess what, friend?" the voice called out.

"What?"

"We got paid in advance," the man said, "and we always earn our money."

Clint wondered how many there were, and if they had the back covered yet. There was only one way to find out. He got off the floor, ran for the back wall and leaped through what was left of a window. When he landed outside he rolled and came up on one knee, holding his gun. When no one fired at him he knew that they had neglected to cover the back—yet. He got up and ran for the trees, hoping to get there unnoticed. Sooner or later somebody would think to cover the back. And he'd be waiting.

"Ain't we been here before?" one man asked.

"Once," another man said.

"Oh, yeah," the first man said. "A necktie party, right? With Walker?"

The third man said, "Both of you shut up about that. Cal, get around to the back. We shoulda done that from the start, except you two geniuses opened fire as soon as you saw him in the doorway."

"Lem," Cal asked, "why we got to do this, anyway? We

got paid, and that rancher feller is in jail. Why don't we just be on our way?"

"Because," Lem Winston said, "if word ever got out we did that we'd never get hired by anybody again. Now go cover the back!"

"All right! Ya don't have ta yell at me."

As Cal started around to cover the back of the house the third man, Del, said, "What a idiot."

"Oh, and you're not?" Lem asked.

"Lem—"

"Just shut up and open fire again. We want to keep him pinned down while Cal gets around back."

The two men opened fire with their carbines.

As the gunfire started again Clint saw the man immediately working his way around to the back, and in doing so was circling right toward Clint's position. He just waited for the man to cross in front of him, then broke cover and jammed his gun into the man's back.

"Wha—"

"Drop the gun."

"You're supposed to be in the house," the man said, as if genuinely puzzled.

"Surprise, surprise," Clint said. "I guess somebody should have thought to cover the back."

The man's gun hit the ground.

"How many out front?"

The man didn't answer right away.

"Why don't I just shoot you now?" He increased the pressure of his gun barrel against the man's back.

"T-two!" the man blurted. "Lem and Del."

"And what's your name?"

"My name is—"

"It doesn't matter what your name is!" Clint said, and clubbed the man over the head. He believed him when he said there were two out front. Considering the other times they had sent men after him, three seemed to be a favorite number.

He picked up the man's gun, tucked it into his belt, and started retracing his steps. Soon enough he came within sight of the other two men, who were reloading their rifles, and apparently arguing.

"I'm jest sayin' ya shouldn't had oughtta call us idiots just 'cause we ain't as smart as you," one of them was saying.

"Just reload, damn it!" the other man said. "I can't help it if you're both stupid."

Clint called out, "Seems to me you're both pretty stupid. Drop your rifles."

The first man hesitated, but the second man swung around, dropped the rifle and went for his gun. Clint drew and fired, hitting the man dead center in the chest. He staggered, coughed up blood, and fell forward onto his face.

The other man convulsively threw his rifle away and put his hands in the air.

"I give up! Don't shoot!"

"Drop your handgun."

The man took it out of his holster and dropped it to the ground.

"Where's my brother Del?"

Well, now he knew the other man's name.

"This one your brother, too?" Clint asked.

"No, just Del. Did you kill him, too?"

"No," Clint said, "you and your brother are still alive, and this one is dead. Who's the idiot now?"

Cal thought about it a moment, then brightened and said, "Yeah!"

"Let's go and collect your brother," Clint said. Seemed he had something to deliver to French Creek other than the gray mare.

Watch for

BARON OF CRIME

223rd novel in the exciting GUNSMITH series
from Jove

Coming in July!